W9-AMB-304

7234115

Thumbprint Mysteries

WITHOUT A TRACE

BY

JUDITH ANDREWS GREEN

CB

CONTEMPORARY BOOKS

a division of NTC/CONTEMPORARY PUBLISHING GROUP
Lincolnwood, Illinois USA

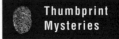

**Thumbprint
Mysteries**

MORE THUMBPRINT MYSTERIES

by Judith Andrews Green:

Hit the Street
Not a Chance

To Torkel

This is a work of fiction. The characters, incidents, and dialogues are products of the author's imagination and are not to be construed as real. Any resemblance to actual events or persons, living or dead, is entirely coincidental.

Cover Illustration: Alan Janson

ISBN: 0-8092-0681-1

Published by Contemporary Books,
a division of NTC/Contemporary Publishing Group, Inc.,
4255 West Touhy Avenue,
Lincolnwood (Chicago), Illinois 60646-1975 U.S.A.
© 1998 Judith Andrews Green

8 9 0 QB 0 9 8 7 6 5 4 3 2 1

CHAPTER 1

It was raining again when Justin Cobb pulled up in front of the day care center to pick up his wife from work. The rain pounded down on the sidewalk, the street, and the hood of his car—a noisy, in-your-face kind of rain. Everything seemed to have had the color washed right out of it, leaving it cold and gray: the buildings, the people on the sidewalk, the cars splashing by on the street. It had been raining for three days. It felt like forever.

Justin was a few minutes late, and he had expected to see Heather waiting in the doorway of the building, ready to go, anxious to get home and get off her feet. But the doorway was empty. *Probably some kid can't find his raincoat*, Justin thought and fiddled with the radio dial.

Minutes passed, and Heather still didn't appear. It wasn't like Heather to be late—that was *his* habit. He really didn't feel like getting wet just to help look for some little kid's raincoat, but he was beginning to feel uneasy.

1

Maybe he'd just run in and check on what was happening.

As he was reaching into the backseat for his jacket, the door of the building opened and a mother and her child scuttled out onto the sidewalk. There was something about the way the woman was holding onto the child, as if she was afraid that the kid would float away like a helium balloon if she let go even for an instant.

The child wanted to stop and splash in a big puddle near the curb, but the woman dragged him away down the sidewalk. Just before they disappeared around the corner, the woman glanced back toward the day care center, and her eyes were round and dark with a mixture of anger and fear.

Something was definitely wrong.

Justin grabbed the jacket, threw it over his head, and dashed for the doorway of the building. He yanked open the faded red door and stepped through.

Into total confusion.

A handful of children huddled over to one side of the room by the coat racks, where a large woman in a bright red blouse was trying to get them to put on their jackets. Several of the children were crying, and one was howling like a lost dog. The toys weren't put away but were still scattered everywhere across the floor. One of the tiny chairs in the story circle lay on its side. Near the door, three mothers gripped their children tightly, as if they couldn't decide whether it was better to stay or to leave.

In the middle of the room, a policeman stood like a tall, blue tree trunk. He was looking down at a short woman in a raincoat and brown hat that made her look like some kind of mushroom.

The woman was screaming.

At Heather.

"I came just as fast as I could!" the woman shrieked. "Oh, what have you done with my poor little Mandy? I thought this was a decent day care center! I thought this was a safe place to leave my child! How could you let this happen?"

"There, there, Mrs. Tate," Heather said when the woman stopped to take a breath. "She hasn't been gone long. I'm sure the police will find her."

"Yes, yes, certainly we'll find her." The policeman's deep voice rumbled like a passing truck below Mrs. Tate's shrieks and the whimpers of the children. "You're the director of the day care center?" he asked Heather.

"Yes," Heather said. Justin could tell by the sound of her voice that she was fighting to stay calm. "My name is Heather Cobb, and I took over as director of the day care center two weeks ago."

"This would never have happened when Mrs. Santos was here!" Mrs. Tate screamed.

Heather glanced over at the mothers hanging onto their children by the doorway. A young man with a ponytail came through the door, took one look at the policeman, and yelled, "Shana! Where are you?" A tiny round girl with a blue ribbon in her hair detached herself from the group at the side of the room, scurried across the floor, and threw herself into his arms.

"Exactly how long has Mandy been missing?" the policeman was asking. "When was the last time you can be sure that she was here?"

"You had her with you at story time, didn't you, Tina?" Heather called to the woman in the red blouse.

"Oh, yes, she was sitting right by me, listening to the story," answered the woman as she straightened up. Short, curly hair surrounded her cheerful face, and she wore bright red lipstick to match the blouse. She had a soft, comfortable look to her, like a favorite pillow.

"Then a lot of people arrived to pick up their children all at once," Heather said, "and with the rain, and all the children needing help with their jackets—"

"There's no excuse for it!" raged Mrs. Tate.

Heather bowed her head. "With all these children getting ready to go at once," she went on, "I guess we lost sight of Mandy. But it can't have been more than a few minutes before we realized she was gone. Right away I sent Nellie out to look for her on the street, and I called the police and then you."

"Nellie is one of your employees?" the policeman asked.

Heather nodded. "Yes, she just came to work here a few days ago. Nellie, could you come out here please?" A slim girl, barely more than a child herself, appeared in the kitchen doorway.

"You went out looking for the missing child?" the policeman asked her.

Nellie turned huge, frightened eyes toward the policeman and gave a tiny nod of her head. The long, dark braid hanging down her back twitched slightly at the movement. Pulling out a small notebook, the policeman walked over and stood looking down at her, until she bent her head toward the floor, hiding her face behind her shoulder. "Where did you look?" the policeman asked.

"Around the block," Nellie said to the floor in a small, childlike voice. "Up two blocks. Down three blocks. In the alley. Then Mrs. Cobb told me to come in."

"Humph!" Mrs. Tate snorted under the brown hat. "Some search that was!"

"She's been on the phone in the kitchen," Heather

explained, "calling all the families who picked up their children this afternoon, to see if anyone saw her go out."

Mrs. Tate wasn't listening. It seemed as if something new had occurred to her, something dreadful, for her eyes bulged, and the blood drained out of her face. She yanked the brown hat off her head and began squeezing it between her hands, crying, "Oh, no, I know what's happened! Her father has snatched her away from me!"

"Her father?" the policeman asked.

"This is all your fault!" Mrs. Tate screamed at Heather. "Just last week I made it very clear to you that you were not to allow Mandy's father to pick her up! Until the divorce is final, I have complete custody of Mandy! And now look what you've done! You've let her father take her, and they're probably headed out of the city right this minute in that darned truck of his! He'll probably head across the country, and he'll hide her away, and I'll never see her again!" Mrs. Tate began to sob. "Oh, my darling, my poor little girl—"

"Daddy, I want to go home!" cried the little girl in the blue ribbon. One after the other, the children began to sniffle, until the whole room echoed with weeping, like the rain falling out on the street.

*   *   *

It was late by the time Heather and Justin got home. Heather looked pale and drawn as Justin sat her down in her favorite chair and made her put her feet up. Then he hurried over to the refrigerator to see if there were any leftovers he could heat up for supper.

"That poor little girl!" Heather sighed. "I certainly felt better when Mrs. Tate finally figured out that Mandy's father had taken her. At least we know she's safe. I've met the father—he used to pick Mandy up sometimes, before he and his wife broke up—and he seemed like a nice enough man."

For a moment Heather sat quietly until the aching questions dragged her to her feet again. "But how on earth did Mr. Tate get in and take her away without our seeing him?"

"Heather, darling, you need to rest!" Justin said. "You know what the doctor said!" He put his arms around her and pulled her to him. "You've got to think of the baby. The police will take care of finding Mandy and her father. But you're the only one who can take care of our baby." He smiled down at her and patted her swelling stomach. "Now come and sit down."

Heather resisted his gentle push toward the chair. "What am I going to do about the day care center? You saw how the parents were looking at me while the policeman was there! If some of them don't bring their kids back again, the day care center will go broke!"

"It's not your fault if—" Justin began.

"But I'm responsible for the children!" She walked heavily over to the window and stood looking down at the street. "And what's going to happen when I have the baby? How can I leave Tina and Nellie in charge? They're both new—they don't know how to run things!"

"Tina seems to know what she's doing," Justin said.

"Oh, Tina's all right, I think. She's always happy and cheerful, and she keeps the children busy. Mrs. Santos knew what she was doing when she hired Tina. But I was the one who hired Nellie, and I think I made a big mistake."

"Why?" Justin asked. He was digging around in the refrigerator, but there didn't seem to be anything he knew how to cook. "What's wrong with Nellie?"

"She's so quiet! She never talks to the parents. She won't even look at them, and that makes them nervous. Did you see her today when the policeman was talking to her? She always looks away, as if she has something to hide."

"There's some hamburger in here," Justin said. "Maybe I could make spaghetti." Holding the refrigerator door open as if he were showing her the contents, he turned to look at Heather. "Do I fry the meat before I put it in the sauce?"

Heather sighed. "Move over," she said.

*   *   *

After supper, Heather called the police department. No, Mandy had not been found. She tried again before she went to bed and again first thing in the morning. No, no sign of Mandy or her father, the police told her. He wasn't at the apartment where he had been staying, and no one had seen him in several days. The landlord thought he might have left town.

Heather hung up the phone and stood at the kitchen window staring out at the rain, which shone like silver in the early morning light. At the table, Justin sat with his second cup of coffee cooling at his elbow. "You wait and wait for spring," he said, just to break the silence, "and all it does is rain."

"I think I'd better get over to the day care center," Heather said.

"Oh, come on, you don't have to open the place for almost an hour!" Justin reminded her. He took a sip of coffee, then made a face. "This stuff is cold. I think I'll just put it in the microwave for a moment. I can fix you a cup of tea—"

"Justin, I want to go now."

"All right, all right." Justin pushed the coffee cup away and stood up. "I'm sure I can find something to do at work. You know darned well that nobody will be buying any cars in this kind of weather. Even if there isn't a soul in the showroom, the boss likes to have all his salesmen lined up as if we think a whole crowd of customers will pop through the door at any moment."

Heather pulled on her raincoat, tried to button it over her stomach, then gave up and let the coat hang open. "Here comes the fat lady, looking for the circus," she said.

It was their favorite joke, and Justin tried to laugh, but today somehow nothing seemed funny. "Honey, you hardly got any sleep all night," he said, making one more attempt. "You should stay home and rest. What can you do at the day care center at this hour?"

"I just want to be there," Heather said.

*   *   *

Justin fetched their car from its parking space in the alley and pulled it up in front of their apartment building. Heather wedged herself into the passenger seat and pulled the door shut. They pulled out into the steady stream of traffic and drove the eight blocks to the day care center in heavy silence.

As they pulled up in front of the day care building, they saw a man standing in the doorway, sheltered from the rain, shoulders hunched against the cold morning air, hands shoved deep into his pockets. He had been peering in through the front window of the day care center, but when the car pulled up he spun around to face them.

As Heather looked out at the man through the car window, her hands flew up and grasped the front of her raincoat. "Oh, my God," she whispered.

"What's the matter?" Justin demanded. "Who is that?"

"That's Mr. Tate," Heather said. "Mandy's father."

CHAPTER 2

"Heather, that man could be dangerous!" Justin said. "Let me handle this! Don't get out of the car!"

But Heather had already opened the car door and heaved herself out onto the sidewalk. "Mr. Tate, do you have Mandy?" she asked.

The man stepped forward into the rain and glared down at her. "I want to know what's going on!" he snapped. "You work here, don't you?"

"Yes, I'm Heather Cobb. I'm the director of the day care center."

"The director?" The man raised one eyebrow as he looked down at her. His eyes traveled down to her rounded stomach sticking out of the open raincoat, and he snorted angrily. "Where's Mrs. Santos?" he demanded.

"Mrs. Santos is not here anymore," Heather said, giving the raincoat a yank in a useless attempt to close it. She

9

took a deep breath, stuck her chin out, and stared straight up at Mr. Tate. "Mrs. Santos left two weeks ago, and as the new director I would like to know if you have taken Mandy."

"That's what I'm here about!" The tendons in the man's neck bunched and knotted like ropes above the open collar of his jacket as he bellowed into Heather's face, "Where's my daughter?"

"Now see here!" Justin rushed around the hood of the car and grabbed the man's arm. "You just back off, buddy!"

The man threw Justin's hand off his arm and swung around toward him, his meaty fists clenched and ready. Then suddenly his anger seemed to disappear, and he crumpled like a piece of wet paper in the rain. "Please," he begged Heather, "please tell me where my little Mandy is!"

"Maybe we should go inside," Heather said. "We can talk better if we're out of the rain." She dug a ring of keys out of her raincoat pocket, unlocked the faded red door, and led the way into the building. When she turned on the lights, the tiny chairs and the little tricycles and the blocks and dolls all seemed to jump to attention, lined up waiting for the children to arrive.

Heather took off her raincoat and hung it on a hook, then sat down in one of the tiny chairs. "If you sit down, Mr. Tate," she said, "and tell me what you know, maybe together we can figure out what has happened to Mandy."

Mr. Tate lowered himself into a chair and sat looking very uncomfortable with his knees pressed against his shoulders. "I was away on my route," he explained. "I drive a tractor-trailer rig and sometimes I'm gone for days. When I got back late last night, there were all these messages on my answering machine—my wife, calling me again and again, screaming something about Mandy. There must have been twenty calls on that tape."

He passed a huge hand slowly over a face that sagged with worry and fatigue. "My wife and I haven't been getting along very well lately," he went on. "To tell you the truth, we're getting a divorce. I guess she thought I came here yesterday afternoon and took Mandy away. But like I said, I was gone on my route, and I didn't know anything about it until I got home about three o'clock this morning."

He looked up at Heather, and tears glinted in his eyes. "Mrs. Cobb, where is my Mandy? Her mother and I may have our differences, but we both love Mandy very much. She's everything to us. Please, what has happened to our Mandy?"

Heather reached forward and put her hand on the man's rain-dampened sleeve. "I'm sorry, Mr. Tate. I just wish I knew."

*   *   *

It was an endless, dreary morning at the Little Friends Day Care Center. The children seemed quiet and subdued, whether from the events of the afternoon before or from the long days of rain, Heather didn't know. And the children weren't all there. As she had feared, three of the families hadn't brought their children in at the regular time. Only one mother had called with an explanation. Heather found herself watching the other parents as they dropped their children off, wondering what they were thinking, wondering if tomorrow their children would be at other day care centers too.

Justin phoned her when he arrived at the car showroom to make sure that Mr. Tate hadn't come back to make any trouble. "Don't worry, he's gone," Heather said. "Look, I can't talk now. Three children are being dropped off at once, and I really need to be there in case the parents have questions."

The front door of the day care center flew open again, admitting a gust of wind and rain and a large woman in a glossy raincoat. "I'm from the Department of Children's Services," she announced as she swept into the room, "and I'm here to investigate the disappearance of—" She snapped open a leather briefcase, pulled out a file folder, consulted a sheet of paper, and continued, "—the disappearance of Mandy Tate."

The woman asked all the same questions that Heather had been through with the police, and then put the same list of questions to Tina, as if she wasn't satisfied with Heather's answers. Tina was carefully showing her the story circle when Nellie appeared at Heather's elbow. "It's Mr. Cobb on the phone for you."

"Oh, Nellie, tell him I'm too busy. I'll call him later when things settle down."

She glanced toward the door, which had just swung open to admit a nervous-looking young man with a large camera slung around his neck. "I'm from the *Herald Gazette*," he said timidly, "and I'd like to talk to Mrs. Cobb."

Heather sent the reporter to talk to Tina, while she answered the child welfare woman's questions all over again. Meanwhile, a second reporter had arrived and was taking photographs of three small girls hunkered down on the floor, getting their dolls ready for bed. When the child welfare woman stalked into the kitchen to check on the facilities, Nellie scuttled past her in the doorway and drifted over to Heather. "Mrs. Cobb," she whispered, staring down at the floor as if there was something very interesting stuck between the cracks in the worn floorboards.

"What is it now, Nellie?" Heather snapped.

"I'm sorry, Mrs. Cobb, you told me to make toasted cheese sandwiches for lunch today, but we don't have enough cheese."

"What do you mean, we don't have enough cheese?" Heather asked, irritated. "There should be plenty of cheese. We don't even have all the kids here today!"

"There's just one package," Nellie said so quietly that Heather almost had to read her lips. "I've looked everywhere."

"Well, as soon as Madame Bigshot from the Department of Children's Services gets out of here, I'll get you some money out of my office and you can go to the store for another package!"

Nellie nodded, turned with a sweep of the black braid, and slid back into the kitchen. As Heather watched her go, something tugged at her memory. Something important.

Then she remembered. Yesterday, while she was preparing for snack time in the afternoon, Nellie had told her that they had run out of juice. Heather had sent her to the store for more.

It was just a few minutes after Nellie got back with the juice that they had realized Mandy was missing.

"Nellie," Heather called. Her mouth was suddenly so dry that the word came out in a croak. "Nellie, never mind the toasted cheese sandwiches. Find something else to cook for lunch!"

*   *   *

Morning slowly turned into afternoon at Manning's Luxury Auto Sales, and afternoon slowly slid toward evening. There had been almost no customers all day, and the mood in the brightly lit showroom was glum to the point of misery.

Justin had spent hour after hour pushing the paperwork from one side of his desk to the other, attempting to look busy, wondering what was going on with Heather. Now he stood in the showroom window, staring out at the rain which whisked across the wet pavement in wind-driven streaks. The new Corvettes, unsold, sat silently in a row of identical shapes, useless. The names of their colors ticked through Justin's brain: *Silver Ghost, Fiesta Red, Blue-Black, Sagebrush.*

He sighed and turned away from the window, asking himself if he was just bored or if he was actually going nuts.

How had it come to this? Two years ago he was a bicycle messenger, zipping through the city in all kinds of weather, cutting in and out of traffic, taking chances, beating the clock. Doing what he loved to do. Free as a bird.

Now look at him: moping around an empty showroom among the fancy sports cars, waiting for customers to come in so that he could give *them* the keys and let *them* pull out into traffic and see what the cars would do.

He'd given up the bicycle job because Heather thought it was too dangerous. Well, it probably *was* too dangerous for a family man, especially the day some guy had chased him in a black Jaguar and tried to flatten him into the pavement. He'd had a thing about Jaguars ever since. They always seemed to be looking at him.

At least he'd been on his own back then. He'd taken his chances against the black Jaguar because he had to keep the guy away from Heather.

Back then, Justin had been able to protect Heather. Now Heather needed help, and there was nothing Justin could do. She wouldn't even return his phone calls!

"Hey, Cobb! Since it seems that you have nothing to do," said a gruff voice behind him as if someone had read his mind, "why don't you go out back and help with the load of pre-owned cars that's just come in?"

Justin spun around to face his boss, a tall, thin man with a permanent worry line etched between his eyebrows. "Yes, sir, Mr. Manning. Any special instructions?"

"Well, the driver's got the first car off the carrier already. I want you to bring it into the showroom and put it right here in the front window. I was lucky—I got a really good deal on it, and it should bring a good price. I'm going to spotlight it in our advertising this week."

"Yes, sir, Mr. Manning."

"Don't forget to dry it off before you bring it onto the polished floor!" Mr. Manning added.

Justin felt his insides twist into a knot. "I'll be sure to take care of it, sir," he said carefully. Then he turned on his heel and headed briskly for the back of the showroom.

"You'll see the car just outside the back door," Mr. Manning called after him. "It's a black Jag."

Justin's steps slowed suddenly. *A black Jaguar!*

Aware of Mr. Manning's eyes on his back, Justin forced himself to walk across the showroom floor to the back door, open the door, and step out into the wet parking lot. The car hunched facing him, gleaming in the rain like some sleek black metallic cat.

The car's door closed with a quiet *snick* as Justin settled himself into the seat. The interior of the car was dry and cool and smelled of fresh paint and newly cleaned upholstery. *It's just a car,* Justin told himself as he turned the key in the ignition, *just a used car.* But as the engine purred into life, the hair stood up along his arms and the back of his neck.

He couldn't help it. Somehow the car felt like an omen.

As if the car was telling him that the bad luck at the Little Friends Day Care Center was about to spread out and take over their lives.

*   *   *

The ride home that evening was very quiet. In the flickering light from the passing streetlights, Heather looked exhausted, drained of all her strength. When Justin squeezed her hand, she didn't squeeze back.

When they got to their apartment building, the silence was over. Mrs. Grasso, their landlady, was waiting for them in the front hall.

"Oh, that poor little girl!" Mrs. Grasso wailed, the moment she caught sight of Heather. "I've been reading all about it in the newspaper!"

She grasped Heather's arm in both her chubby hands and pulled her toward the open door of her apartment. "I saw your name—Mrs. Heather Cobb, director—and I thought to myself, but that's *our* Heather! Poor Heather will be so tired she won't know which end is up, and she'll need some supper. So I've made some nice lasagna for you and Justin. It's all ready. Just come right in and sit yourselves down, both of you!"

A heavenly mixture of smells wafted down the hallway from Mrs. Grasso's doorway: fresh bread, cheese melting, and Mrs. Grasso's special homemade tomato sauce, which Justin knew would be rich with sausage and enough garlic to make his throat tingle. He knew that Heather probably just wanted to have a cup of herbal tea and go straight to bed, but they couldn't pass up Mrs. Grasso's lasagna!

Heather allowed herself to be dragged along the narrow hallway. "That's so nice of you," she murmured when Mrs. Grasso stopped talking for a moment to catch her breath. "That's so very nice of you."

Mrs. Grasso's little black poodle was waiting for them in the doorway like an electric doormat. He danced around them, jumping up to put his tiny feet against Heather's legs, then dashing over to growl a tiny growl at Justin, then back to beg for a pat from Heather. "Now,

now, Clarence, be a good boy," Mrs. Grasso said as she scooped him up in her arms and swept Heather and Justin through the door into her apartment.

Moments later they were tucked up to the little square table in Mrs. Grasso's kitchen. Their places were already set with silverware and paper napkins, and Mrs. Grasso set a big basket of warm bread in the middle of the table before turning to draw an enormous pan of lasagna out of the oven.

"Can I help you with that?" Justin asked, his mouth already full of bread.

"No, no, everything's ready, you just eat!" Mrs. Grasso sang out. She cut huge portions of lasagna and transferred them onto the waiting plates. She turned toward the table with the plates held high next to her head, on either side of her wide smile. "You poor, tired children, you just eat!"

Justin dug in happily, but across from him Heather just picked around the edges of her food. Mrs. Grasso clucked sympathetically and patted Heather's shoulder. "It's a big problem for you, isn't it?" she asked.

Heather nodded. "I'm just so upset about Mandy. She's such a little spitfire and just as smart as she could be. She's only four years old, but she already knows all her letters." Heather sighed. "She was such a happy little girl when she first came to the day care center. But then her parents started having problems, and she began to be very quiet. Lately she's been spending a lot of time just sitting in the corner."

Heather set down her fork and wiped away a tear. "I think her parents were fighting all the time, and it really bothered her. Oh, it's just not fair, what these kids go through! I just can't stand it!"

"But how did it happen?" Mrs. Grasso asked, sitting

down at the table. "Did someone come in and get her, or did she just open the door and run away?"

"I've thought and thought and thought about it," Heather said. "A lot of people came in at once, and they all seemed to be in such a hurry to pick up their children and get home. I'm sure they were all people that we knew. Just our regular families—mothers and fathers, and some older sisters and brothers, picking up the kids the way they do every day."

She laid her fork down again next to her almost untouched plate and folded her napkin. "We called all the families yesterday to see if Mandy had gone home with someone by mistake. We talked to them again today. All except the three that didn't show up." She picked up her napkin again and crunched it in her hand.

"The Scarpellis called in to say that Mona was sick, although she seemed fine when she went home yesterday. But the Hoffmans and Mrs. Ripley didn't even bother to call. They just didn't show up." She looked down at the napkin in her hand, saw that it was now reduced to a tiny white wad of paper, and stuck it into her pocket. "By the end of the week I'll bet we'll have only a few kids left."

Mrs. Grasso's dark eyes were suddenly sharp in the soft folds of her face. "They just didn't show up?" she asked in a tight, hard voice, very different from her usual bird-like chirp. "Heather, I think we've got to find a way to get into those homes and find out what's going on!"

"But, Mrs. Grasso, I really don't think—" Heather protested.

Suddenly there was a loud knock on the door. Clarence leapt off his pillow in the corner and ran around the table, yapping.

Mrs. Grasso jumped up to peer through the peephole, then turned around to beam at them. "You'll never guess who's here!" she said. "And he's just the person we need. I think I'm beginning to have a great idea!"

CHAPTER 3

Mrs. Grasso unhooked the chain lock and threw open the door. Standing in the doorway, blinking in the sudden light from the kitchen, was a thin young man with a neon green knit cap pulled down over one eyebrow. His long hair poked out from under the cap in various directions. His baggy blue jeans and rumpled red plaid lumberjack shirt looked as if he had slept in them for a week before being caught out in the rain.

The young man pulled off his cap, ran his hand over his head as if to make sure it was still there, and grinned at Justin and Heather. "*Here* you are!" he said. "I thought I'd find you here!"

"Hugo!" Justin said. "I haven't seen you in ages! Where have you been keeping yourself?"

"Oh, here and there," Hugo said. His soggy high-top sneakers squelched as he walked across the kitchen floor to give Heather a noisy kiss on the cheek. "So, Heather,

19

you're getting big! How are things with the mother of my future godchild?"

Heather smiled in spite of herself. "Hello, Hugo, we've missed you. Life is just too normal when you're not around."

"I'll take that as a compliment, I think," Hugo said, plopping himself down in the chair where Mrs. Grasso had been sitting. He reached down to pat the dog, who was wagging his tail so hard that he was almost bending himself in two. Then Hugo leaned over Justin's plate of lasagna and breathed in. "Boy, that smells good!"

Mrs. Grasso stopped clucking over the muddy footprints Hugo had left across her clean linoleum and hurried to the kitchen cupboard for another plate. Soon Hugo was digging into a double serving of lasagna while Mrs. Grasso put the water on to boil for coffee.

"I saw in the newspaper about the kid who got lost out of your day care center," Hugo said around a mouthful of lasagna, "and I knew you'd be upset. So I thought I'd come around and try to cheer you up." He grinned a tomato-sauce grin.

Heather set her elbow on the edge of the table and leaned her chin into the palm of her hand. Her eyes sagged shut. "If *Hugo* knows about Mandy's disappearance, then everyone in the city knows about it!" she said.

Mrs. Grasso set four cups in a row along the counter and spooned instant coffee into them. "I've got it all figured out! Just listen to my plan." She poured boiling water into the cups and carted them to the table. "See, you've got three families who have just disappeared without asking for their money back. That's not normal. The best way to check them out—"

"Is to send the police?" Heather suggested.

"No, if the police show up, whoever's got Mandy will

hide her for sure! No, we send someone they'll never suspect. We send Hugo. He can pretend to be a census taker. He can go see each family, knock on the door, and ask to have a look at everyone who lives there!"

"Well, I do have their home addresses here in my bag . . ." Heather admitted.

Heather's eyes had lost that look of total exhaustion, Justin noticed. It would be worth going along with this crazy idea just to make her happy. "Okay," he said, "but I should be the one to go. Heather's the director of the day care center, and she's *my* wife!"

"Exactly!" Mrs. Grasso said. "People have seen you taking Heather to work. They know you!"

"Sounds like fun!" Hugo said. He shoveled the last of his lasagna into his mouth, washed it down with his coffee, picked up his green cap, and asked, "When do I start?"

"What time does the cat say?" Mrs. Grasso glanced up at the wall clock, which was in the shape of a cat with a tail that swung back and forth to mark the passing seconds. "Well, it's already 7:45, but if we hurry, we can go tonight!" She watched Hugo settle the green cap back onto his hair, which looked as if it was fighting back, and shook her head. "You're going to need some fixing up, I think."

Justin sighed loudly and stood up. "I'll go upstairs and get him some clothes," he said. "I've got some stuff that would fit him."

"Get him some shoes too," Mrs. Grasso said, pointing with disgust at his soggy footwear. Hugo's big toe waved back through a huge hole in the side of his right sneaker. "And some socks."

"Not your new brown shoes," Heather called after him, "and not your good suit, either!" Her eyes darted over to Hugo and she added, "No offense, Hugo."

Hugo shrugged. "No problem. While we're waiting, Mrs. Grasso, is there any more of that wonderful lasagna?"

*   *   *

Dressed in Justin's second-best suit and armed with the briefcase that Heather had given Justin for his birthday, Hugo set out into the night with Mrs. Grasso as his chauffeur. Justin and Heather were elected to stay in Mrs. Grasso's apartment and keep the dog company. "Poor Clarence gets so lonely when he's here by himself," Mrs. Grasso explained, but everyone knew that it was just a good excuse to get Heather to sit down and rest.

An hour ticked by on the cat clock. Heather sat with her eyes closed, looking pale. Justin paced up and down between the kitchen window and the peephole on the door. He couldn't believe that he'd let Hugo go out and work on this, while he had to stay home and baby-sit a stupid dog. What was happening to him?

Suddenly Heather's eyes popped open. "You're driving me crazy!" she snapped. "If you can't sit still, why don't you take the dog for a walk?"

"That dog! He won't come with me! He hates me! Mrs. Grasso's old dog hated me, and now this one does too! Why me? And the old lady's weird, naming a dog after her dead husband!"

Heather closed her eyes again. "Clarence is a better name than Fifi. Take him for a walk."

"All right, I will," Justin said. And as soon as he found the leash where it hung tidily on a hook by the door, the dog actually came right to him, wagging his tail. In a moment, he and the dog were out on the wet sidewalk in a cold rain that immediately began to work its way under his jacket collar.

The dog pulled on the leash, trying to investigate some

smelly bit of trash in the gutter. He was surprisingly strong for such a tiny beast. "Come on, you foolish animal!" Justin growled, yanking on the leash until the dog turned and trotted along beside him down the sidewalk.

They circled the block twice before Justin felt wet and cold enough to want to be back inside Mrs. Grasso's overly warm kitchen. The dog seemed to be perfectly happy out there in the rain, sniffing at trash cans and phone poles and anything else he could wrap the leash around. But as they came back toward their own front door, the dog broke into a run that looked as if someone was bouncing him up and down on a string. *What's with this idiot dog?* Justin wondered. Then he saw Mrs. Grasso's car coming toward them down the street. As Mrs. Grasso steered the car oh-so-carefully into the alley to park it, Hugo grinned triumphantly at Justin through the passenger window.

Justin dragged the dog up the front steps into the hallway and kicked the front door shut behind him. "Don't make so much noise!" Mrs. Grasso called from her apartment doorway. "You'll bother everyone in the building!"

Justin let the dog run to her and followed the dragging leash into her apartment. Heather was sitting forward in her chair, her eyes fixed on Hugo. Justin looked away and asked in a harsh voice, "Any luck?"

"First we have to dry off my poor little precious baby," Mrs. Grasso said, wrapping the dog up in a huge fluffy towel printed all over with large pink roses. "Mama's poor little fellow out in the wet and cold without his little jacket on!"

Justin glanced over at the door. Sure enough, there was a little blue dog jacket hanging next to the hook where the leash had been. Oh, well!

Hugo laid the briefcase on the kitchen table and

unloaded the paper and pencils he had taken along. His face was full of importance, as if Justin's second-best suit had turned him into a wealthy banker. Actually, he didn't look half bad—except for his hair, which was already trying to escape from the rubber band that Heather had used to pull it back into a ponytail.

"Okay, okay," Mrs. Grasso said, "everyone sit down. Now, Hugo, tell us what you found out."

Hugo cleared his throat, placed the papers in a neat pile, took one paper out of the middle of the stack and put it on the top, then cleared his throat again. "Well," he said, "you wanted me to visit the three families who did not bring their children to the Little Friends Day Care Center today."

"Yes, yes!" Heather cried. "For God's sake, Hugo, what did you find out? Did you see Mandy?"

"Well, let's see." He picked up the top paper, then put it to one side and picked up another sheet. "Um, first I went to see the Scarpelli family. There was a Gino Scarpelli, that's the father, and a Rosa Scarpelli, that's the mother, and a Mrs. Fabio, I think she was Mrs. Scarpelli's mother."

"What about the kids?" Heather begged. "They've got two kids at the day care center, Mona and Maria."

Hugo consulted his paper. "Yes, they said they have two children, aged three and four. There was also a young man there who didn't give his name. He said he didn't live there. His English wasn't very good."

"But you didn't see the children?" Heather asked.

"No, they were in bed already."

"Oh," Mrs. Grasso said, "I thought you told me you saw them." Her shoulders slumped as she added, "Maybe we should have waited until tomorrow after all."

"What about the other families?" Heather asked.

Hugo shuffled through the papers again. "Let's see . . . I also visited the Hoffmans. I think that was the place. There were a lot of people when I got there. It was pretty noisy. There were three or four men eating in the kitchen, a bunch of women talking, and all kinds of kids running around. I asked which ones lived there, and . . . let's see . . ."

He looked at one paper, then turned it over and looked at the back, then shuffled through the stack again. "I have it here somewhere. There was a Mr. and Mrs. Hoffman, I know that, and some of the kids were hers from a previous marriage, and their last name was—um— I wish I could find the right piece of paper."

"What about Mrs. Ripley, Suzanne's mother?" Heather cut in. "That's the third place you were going to go."

Hugo looked at Mrs. Grasso for help. "They weren't home, right? No, wait! We went back and saw them, and I think it was just the two of them, this Ripley lady and her little boy."

"Suzanne is a girl," Heather said quietly.

Hugo's face crumpled. "Oh, right," he murmured, "a little girl." He stuck his fingers into the rubber band that was holding back his hair and yanked on it until it broke. Then he ran his fingers over the top of his head until his hair stood out in all directions. "I guess I wasn't much help," he said into the silence around the table.

Mrs. Grasso patted his arm. "You did fine for the first attempt," she said, "but I think we have to do some more investigating on these families. Tomorrow they could have a visit from a social worker." She smiled grimly. "Me!"

"Wait!" Justin cried, jumping up and grabbing the briefcase, which dumped a river of papers onto the floor. "I should be the one who goes—"

"No, Justin, please!" Heather said, sinking back in her

chair. "We should leave these poor families alone. They haven't done anything wrong. They're just worried about their children." She looked up at them with eyes reddened by fatigue and worry. "Besides, I think you're investigating in the wrong direction."

"What do you mean?" Mrs. Grasso demanded.

"I think someone should be checking up on Nellie Ramirez," Heather said. "Nellie doesn't say much, but she's always lurking around in the background, watching me—and she doesn't miss anything."

She shook her head. "Ever since Nellie came to work at the day care center, things have been going wrong. Little things. For example, suddenly it seems as if we're always running out of something—milk, or cheese, or crackers, even paper towels. And now there's this business with Mandy, and I can't help wondering if—"

She bent down to pat the dog, which was curled up against her left foot. "I spoke to the police about Nellie this morning, but they didn't think they could really do anything about her. They just said I should keep an eye on her and report anything suspicious." She laughed bitterly. "Right now, *everything* seems suspicious to me!"

Heather grabbed the edge of the table and pulled herself up out of her chair, disrupting the dog. Clarence ran over to his pillow in the corner and flopped down to glare at Justin as if this were all his fault.

"Mandy has been gone for almost thirty hours," she said quietly. She closed her eyes, and tears squeezed out from under the lids. "With every passing hour, there is less and less chance that we will ever see her again alive."

CHAPTER 4

Heather turned and twisted on the bed, trying to sleep. When she did sleep, she cried out with nightmares. Then she got up to wander about the apartment in the dark, looking out the windows at the empty street below, glistening in the rain.

Morning came at last. Before Justin even opened his eyes, he knew that something was different. He lay still for a moment, trying to figure out what it was, then opened his eyes to see a thin stripe of sunlight across the floor. The rain had stopped.

He threw back the covers and jumped up out of bed. Heather was sitting at the kitchen table by the window, drinking a cup of tea and looking out at the early-morning traffic passing below them. The light from the window shone on her hair and on the steam rising around her face from the hot tea. To Justin she looked thin and exhausted and very beautiful.

"Good morning, sweetheart," he called out.

Heather looked up at him without speaking, then turned her face back toward the window. Justin just stood and looked at her. There was nothing he could think of to do or say to help her.

He had never felt so useless.

*   *   *

The day care center's red door looked even more in need of paint in the bright morning sun, when Justin dropped Heather off that morning. "I'll come and paint that for you some evening this week," he said, "as soon as it's good and dry." Heather didn't answer. She levered herself out of the car and disappeared into the building without looking back.

Tina was coming along the sidewalk, lifting her broad face to the sunshine. She flipped Justin a cheery wave as she pulled the door open and stepped inside.

Through the window he caught a glimpse of two large dark eyes, then the movement of the long rope of dark hair. Nellie Ramirez had been watching him through the window, but as soon as he looked at her, she turned away.

Because he could think of nothing better to do, Justin put the car in gear and pulled away from the curb.

*   *   *

By the time he got to the car showroom, Justin knew that he had to do something—anything—to help find Mandy.

He phoned Mrs. Grasso. "I'm going to go with you to visit those families today," he told her. "I'll come by on my lunch hour and pick you up."

"Oh, don't bother. Hugo can help me," Mrs. Grasso said cheerfully. "If you go, they might—"

"I know, they might recognize me. So I'll stay out of

sight. I'll see you at 12:10." He hung up before she could argue any further.

He spent most of the morning showing the black Jaguar to an elderly businessman. While the businessman sat in the driver's seat running his hands over the steering wheel, patting the upholstery, and examining each and every dial on the dashboard, Justin stood by the hood, looking at the car through squinted eyes. He was trying to picture in his mind the Jaguar that had chased him through the city streets, trying to run him over.

What year had that car been? Could this possibly be the same car? What had become of the driver? Justin would probably never know.

He wished that the businessman would buy this car and get it out of the showroom, out of his life. But after the old man had used up more than an hour of his time looking at every inch of the car and asking questions, he toddled out into the bright sunshine and walked away.

By the time his lunch hour came, Justin felt ready to burst out of his skin. When the other salesmen headed down to the deli on the corner, he dashed out to the parking lot and jumped into his car.

Mrs. Grasso was waiting for him on the front steps. "First stop, Mrs. Ripley," she puffed as she wedged herself into the passenger seat of Justin's car. Justin stayed in the car while Mrs. Grasso waddled up the front steps of Mrs. Ripley's building. A few minutes later she was back again.

"What did you find out?" Justin asked.

"Mrs. Ripley was there by herself. She said she'd sent her daughter to the day care center today. I think she has a new boyfriend," Mrs. Grasso whispered. "There was a man there! Maybe they were off somewhere with him yesterday."

"Okay, okay." Justin turned the key in the ignition. He didn't want to lose his whole lunch hour listening to this!

Mrs. Grasso directed him to the Hoffmans' address, which turned out to be on Edgemont Street, a big brick building painted white, with an alley running down the side. He'd been by it often, since it was just a few blocks over from the day care center. Suddenly, he didn't like the looks of the place. "I'm coming in with you," he said.

Mrs. Grasso must have had the same feeling about the building, because she didn't object. With Justin right behind her, she panted up the dark staircase to the second floor, hauling herself up one step at a time by hanging onto the rickety railing. *The old woman's got guts!* Justin thought to himself.

Holding one finger to her lips, Mrs. Grasso pointed at a door opposite the landing. A strip of light gleamed under the door. As Justin paused on the landing, he could hear muffled voices beyond the door, then a quick burst of shuffling footsteps, as if the people were carrying something heavy across the floor inside the apartment.

Mrs. Grasso raised one eyebrow and looked back at Justin, who nodded and stepped back into the deeper shadows of the landing. Mrs. Grasso stepped up to the apartment door and knocked.

Instantly the footsteps inside the apartment stopped. There was no sound except Mrs. Grasso's wheezing breath. It seemed to Justin as if the whole building was stopped, listening. No one came to the door.

Mrs. Grasso knocked again, loudly. The sound reverberated in the hallways and up and down the staircase.

Beyond the door there was a soft grunt, a slight thud, and the gentle rustle of footsteps receding into the further depths of the apartment.

"Hello? Hello?" Mrs. Grasso called. "I'm from the Department of Children's Services! I'd like to speak to Mr. or Mrs. Hoffman!"

There was no sound at all from the apartment.

Mrs. Grasso waited one more long minute, then turned, grasped the railing, and began to lower herself down the stairs.

Careful to match his footsteps to hers, Justin followed. Just as he reached the lower landing, he heard the tiny *snick* of a doorknob turning somewhere above him. He whirled around to look, but in the hallway above there was only darkness and silence.

"Well, what do you make of that?" Mrs. Grasso asked when they were safely back in the car. "There was definitely someone inside that apartment, and they sure didn't want to talk to us. Do you think we should call the police?"

Justin considered for a moment, then shook his head. "What can the police do? It's not against the law to refuse to answer the door. And I'm not sure I want to explain what we were doing here."

Mrs. Grasso shrugged. "Okay, let's go see what the Scarpellis are up to today."

The Scarpellis' apartment, luckily for Mrs. Grasso, was on the first floor of their building five blocks away. But the Scarpellis weren't home. They truly weren't home.

The apartment door stood ajar, revealing an empty room. A worn couch sat by itself on a threadbare carpet. Beyond an open doorway, two beds stood side by side, stripped to the mattresses. In the kitchen, the cupboard doors hung open to show empty shelves. Bits of paper from a quick packing job littered the floor along with a worn-out sock, a doll that was missing an arm, and several soda bottles.

"Looks like they left in a hurry," Justin said.

"Are you looking for an apartment?" asked a voice behind them. An elderly man with bushy white eyebrows was coming toward them down the hall.

"No," Justin said, "we were looking for the Scarpellis."

"Can't help you there," the man said. "They left in the night without a word to me. I'm the building superintendent, you see. They were all paid up to the end of the week, but off they went." He looked up at Justin, and the eyebrows wiggled as if they too were deeply upset with this. "Seemed like nice enough folks, but off they went." The superintendent moved off down the hall, muttering to himself, "You just never know."

Because they couldn't think of anything better, Justin and Mrs. Grasso headed back to their apartment building. They found Hugo waiting for them on the front steps, absentmindedly chewing on a piece of his hair. He jumped up when he saw them and ran down to lean into the passenger side of the car as soon as Mrs. Grasso opened the door. "Where have you been? What have you found out? What's the news?"

"If you'll let me get out, Hugo," Mrs. Grasso grumbled, "I'll fill you in."

"Okay," Hugo said when she had told him about their visits, "so what do we do next?"

Justin and Mrs. Grasso stared at him for a moment, and then at each other, and then at the ground.

Justin found himself remembering Nellie's face peering at him through the window of the day care center. "You know, I think we might find out something if we followed that Nellie Ramirez."

Hugo's face brightened. "I could do that!" he said. "Let me do that! What does she look like?"

Justin looked at him doubtfully. He knew that Hugo felt bad about screwing things up last night—but the chances were pretty good he'd screw this up too. Still, there weren't very many other options. Justin couldn't follow her—she knew him. And poor old Mrs. Grasso wouldn't be able to keep up.

"She's about this high," Justin said, holding his hand above the ground at shoulder height, "and she has dark hair with a long braid down her back. I think she leaves about 5:00, and the other woman, Tina, locks up when the last two children are picked up."

Mrs. Grasso snorted. "Heather certainly couldn't leave Nellie to lock up! Those last two children would disappear off the face of the earth!"

*   *   *

Justin left Hugo and Mrs. Grasso making plans for the afternoon. He still had almost half an hour left before he had to be back at the prison that Mr. Manning called a showroom. Just enough time to stretch out a bit.

He dragged his bicycle from the basement out into the alley. He yanked off his necktie, rolled it up, and stuffed it in his suitcoat pocket. Then he traded his suitcoat and his shoes, which he stuffed into the saddlebag, for a nylon jacket and a pair of sneakers. In a moment he was down the alley and pedaling the bicycle out into traffic.

It felt so good to be out again on the bicycle after all that rain!

He moved down the street, easily at first, keeping pace with the traffic. Then he leaned low over the handlebars and began to move faster, shifting through the gears, enjoying the feel of the wheels rolling on the pavement. He moved up in the flow of traffic, passing between the moving cars and the line of parked cars at the curb. When he came to the intersection, he cut to the right just as the light turned red, and almost laid the bicycle over on its side. He flashed down the next block with the whole lane to himself, far ahead of the next pack of cars.

He shot through the next intersection, dodged around

a delivery truck that was double-parked halfway down the block, and flew down the street, legs pumping, grinning like a fool. He hopped up onto the sidewalk and cut across the corner at the next intersection just for the fun of it. Just like his old days as a bicycle messenger.

Without thinking about where he was going, he zigzagged through several blocks, deciding whether to turn the corner or go straight by how the traffic was moving. Suddenly he realized that he was only two blocks from the day care center. Well, he might as well stop in and tell Heather about his useless trip with Mrs. Grasso.

He whirred smoothly along Randall Street. In the next block, a woman was coming toward the day care center, carrying a large plastic grocery bag. As he came closer, he saw that it was Nellie Ramirez.

As Nellie pulled open the faded red door, she glanced out at the street, at the traffic flowing by. Suddenly the grocery bag slipped out of her hands and crashed to the sidewalk. Her hands flew up to her face. She started screaming.

Justin leaned into the pedals and shot forward, then threw the bicycle over against the curb and grabbed Nellie by the arm. "What's the matter?" he shouted.

"Mandy!" Nellie sobbed. "Mandy Tate was in that truck! I saw her looking out the window! That red pickup truck!" she cried, pointing. "The one going around the corner!"

Justin looked hard at Nellie. Was she telling the truth?

He couldn't wait to find out. The pickup truck had already disappeared from sight. He pulled the bicycle upright and shot away after the truck.

Chapter 5

Justin pedaled as hard as he could toward the end of the block. As he shot around the corner, he glanced back toward the day care center. The sidewalk in front of the red door was empty. Nellie had disappeared.

Where had she gone? Inside the day care center, to get Heather? To call the police? Or somewhere else, to hide? The questions raced through Justin's mind in time with his pedaling feet and his beating heart.

His eyes flicked forward, down the street ahead of him. The red truck, a Dodge Ram, was a block in front of him, moving fast. It was pulling away from the two cars moving behind it, but Justin still couldn't see who was in the Dodge because its bed was loaded high with boxes of some kind, all different shapes and sizes, covered with a blue plastic tarp.

Beyond the truck, at the next intersection, the traffic light turned yellow.

Justin leaned into the pedals, trying to close the distance. As he cut next to the car ahead of him, he willed the Dodge to slow down, to stop at the light. *Oh, come on, come on, light, turn red now!*

The truck pulled through the intersection. Above it, the traffic light turned red.

The pack of cars waiting at the light on the other street began to pull out across the intersection, cutting off his view of the red truck. The car in front of him had stopped, and the one he had passed was closing in behind him again.

Justin didn't even hesitate. From the time his feet had hit the bicycle's pedals, the old instincts from his days as a bicycle messenger had kicked in. The old boss had always told the messengers that they couldn't make time while they waited at traffic lights. The boss had a real thing about waiting for traffic lights. Justin had lots of practice in *not* waiting.

Now, as his bicycle whizzed up to the intersection, Justin's head concentrated on the red truck that was vanishing in the distance. His body's reflexes took over on everything else.

Quick as thought, he cut alongside the car that had stopped in front of him. He slowed his pedaling to pinpoint the timing, then pumped the pedals hard and shot out into the intersection just inches behind a passing car. In the next second he cut left behind a car passing the other way. Horns blared. Somewhere to his left, brakes squealed. But he was through!

He glanced up. Ahead of him, the street was empty.

Where had that truck gone?

He pedaled furiously down the empty lane. To disappear so quickly, the truck must have turned at the next corner while Justin was working his way through the traffic at the intersection. He had to make it to the next corner in time to see which way the truck had gone!

Or were they playing games with him? Had Nellie sent him off on a wild-goose chase while back at the day care center . . . *what was happening?*

Justin tried to shut off his brain. He couldn't be in two places at once! He had to do his best here. He pumped his pedals as fast as the wheels would turn, but already his legs were feeling the long winter of staying indoors most of the time.

The corner came at him. He slewed to the right, jammed on the brakes with a thin squeal, and gazed down the street.

No truck. Cars and delivery trucks and a few people on the sidewalks, but no red pickup truck.

Behind him, cars were coming at him down the street. He jerked himself around and looked up the street. No pickup truck in that direction, either.

A horn honked, then honked again, louder. A car squeezed around him, revving its engine like a huge, angry insect. A delivery truck pulled up behind him, and the driver leaned out the window and shouted, "Nice trick back there, buddy! You almost caused an accident! What are you, crazy? For crying out loud, get out of the street!"

Justin glanced back at the driver without really seeing him, then hitched the bicycle up onto the curb. The red Dodge had to be somewhere! His mind raced through the possibilities as if they were side streets. Somehow he knew that the clue was right in front of him, if he could only see it!

Then he had it. He looked up at the street sign over his head: yes, he was on Edgemont Street.

Halfway down the block was the white brick building with the alley running along the side. The building where the Hoffmans lived.

Well, he would have to check it out.

He got back on the bicycle and pedaled down the street at what he hoped would look like a normal, don't-mind-me-I'm-just-passing-by sort of speed. As he passed the brick building, he cranked his eyes around so that he could look down the alley without turning his head.

No one seemed to be about. The alley was empty right across the block, like looking through a hollow tube.

He rode down to the end of the block, well out of sight of the brick building, and stopped to think. Probably the red truck didn't have anything to do with the Hoffmans. There were other alleys, other side streets, a whole city it could have disappeared into.

He glanced at his wristwatch. His lunch hour was over. He should be in his car right this minute, headed back to Old Man Manning's House of Boredom. He grasped the bicycle's handlebars, turned them toward home, and pushed off around the corner.

He turned another corner at the end of the block, and a moment later he realized he was passing the other end of the alley that ran past the Hoffmans' building. As if it had a mind of its own, the bicycle turned into the alley, with Justin along for the ride.

He pedaled slowly up the alley, past garages and back doors and garbage dumpsters and parked cars—but no red pickup truck. No one was around. The only movement was an orange tiger cat that crossed the alley on silent feet, carrying its tail high like a flag.

Up ahead there was a pair of garages with sagging ridgepoles and warped, battered doors. Beyond the

garages Justin could see the back of the brick building—
not white back here, as if the white paint was only for
show out front. Between the building and the garages
was a narrow space containing a few garbage cans
crammed with empty cardboard boxes that looked as if
they had been flattened by someone jumping on them,
and a motorcycle covered with a black cloth.

It was the motorcycle that made Justin stop. Why
would someone leave a motorcycle out in the alley in the
middle of the city, when there was a nice, safe garage
right there?

He glanced back at the garages. The windows in the
overhead doors, which had been broken out, had been
replaced with plywood nailed to the inside. The doors
themselves were pulled tight down to the ground. Justin
glanced around to be sure that the alley was still clear
and that no faces had appeared in any of the windows of
the brick building. Then he tried the handle on the
nearer garage door. It was securely locked.

He pushed the bicycle back around the further garage,
out of sight of the brick building, and leaned it against
the splintered, drooping clapboards. The back of the
garage was a solid wall, but the side had a small window
up high under the peak of the roof. The cloth covering
the window on the inside had ripped along one side,
leaving a narrow gap next to the window frame. Justin
stared up at the hole, but all he could see was the rafters
holding up the garage roof.

He needed something to stand on. He looked around
him, but the only thing he could think of was one of the
garbage pails full of cardboard—and he didn't think it
would be wise to draw attention to himself by stealing a
garbage pail right out from under the Hoffmans' windows.

At last he pushed his bicycle directly under the garage

window and wedged it as tightly as he could into the dirt, which was still wet from the days of rain. Hanging onto the splits and breaks in the clapboards for support, he clambered onto the bicycle pedal, and then onto the frame. The bicycle rolled slightly, making him grasp in panic at the window frame.

He put his face up to the hole in the window covering and peered inside the garage. It was dark inside after the bright sunlight of the alley, and it took a moment for his eyes to get adjusted well enough that he could see.

The garage seemed to be full of rectangular shapes of all sizes, piled one on top of the other—cardboard boxes, he guessed. There were several hundred of them, filling most of the floor space of the garage. At the far end of the garage some empty boxes lay jumbled and broken, ready, he supposed, to be taken outside. He strained to read the lettering stenciled on the boxes nearer to the window, but there wasn't enough light. *This must be some kind of warehouse*, he said to himself. There was no sign of the red truck—and no sign of Mandy Tate. He sighed. *False alarm, I guess. It was worth a try.*

He began to turn away from the window, balancing on the frame of the bicycle, preparing himself to jump down.

A large hand closed around his ankle.

"Hey!" he squawked. He grabbed for the window frame, desperately trying to keep his balance. The bicycle shifted in the soft dirt and slid out from under him. He came down with a crash across the metal frame. The handlebar took him in the jaw like a fist. At the same moment, the upper pedal slammed into his ribs and the wind went out of him with a whoosh. He lay dazed in a tangle of arms and legs and metal frame.

"And just what do you think you're doing, snooping around here?" a voice snarled.

Justin twisted his head against the handlebar, trying to see where the voice was coming from.

Then his eyes focused on a pair of legs.

Large legs, covered with dark green work pants and ending in heavy boots.

He hoped the boots weren't going to kick him.

"I said, what are you doing here?" the voice boomed again.

Justin fought to get air into his lungs against the heaving of his ribs. At last he managed to draw a breath, figure out where his arms were, and push himself up out of the bicycle frame. He looked up at the two men whirling above him and struggled to put them together into one man standing still. The man was younger than Justin, hardly more than a kid, but he was huge, and he looked as if he knew how to use his size. "I was just—I was just passing by," Justin gasped, "and I guess I fell—"

"Just passing by, huh?" the man snorted. "What were you doing, looking in the window?"

"What's going on over there?" another voice shouted before Justin could think of an answer. "Who are you talking to?"

"I caught this guy looking in the window, boss," called out the man standing over Justin. "He was standing on a bicycle so that he could see in."

A second man stalked across the alley and stood looking down at Justin. He was in his thirties, well over six feet tall but skinny, with large, callused hands. His face was long and thin, and his eyes had dark circles under them. He looked deeply unhappy.

"I don't know, Mack," he said slowly. "If it's not one thing around here, it's another. This whole operation seems to be going down the tubes. Ever since Lisa screwed everything up the other day, everything just seems to go wrong."

The man named Mack nodded in agreement. "I don't know how this guy got onto us. Everything's clean and out of sight, just like you said."

"What about that?" the other man asked, pointing at the flattened cardboard boxes around the garbage pails. "For crying out loud, that right there is enough to give us away." He sighed. "Well, I guess you'd better bring him inside. I've got some rope. We can tie him up while we figure out how to get rid of him." The man pulled a set of keys out of his pocket, strode over to the other garage, and unlocked the overhead door.

As the door rose, the sun flashed on red paint: the back end of a pickup truck.

Mack reached down to grab Justin by the back of his collar and yanked him to his feet in one motion. Justin staggered, trying to keep his balance, while the world spun around him for a moment.

"Get him over here," the other man snapped. "We've got to get him out of sight!"

Mack gave Justin a shove in the direction of the garage. "We're coming, Mr. Hoffman," he said.

CHAPTER 6

When Nellie burst into the day care center without the groceries she'd been sent to buy, Heather wanted to fire her on the spot.

The way they kept running out of things the last few days, she was pretty sure that Nellie was stealing food out of the kitchen, although she hadn't been able to catch her doing it. She hated having to give Nellie money to go to the store, but they needed the things, and after Mandy's disappearance, she didn't dare leave Nellie alone with the children.

But this was the last straw. Here was Nellie, acting strange, with no groceries in her hands—and the money gone too. This was it!

"Mrs. Cobb! Mrs. Cobb, please come here!" Nellie was pulling at her arm, trying to drag her into the office.

"Nellie, let go of me! I won't have you acting like this in front of the children! You were supposed to be getting the juice for the children's snack and some butter too. Now where are those groceries?"

"They're out on the sidewalk. Mrs. Cobb, I think—"

"Out on the sidewalk!" Heather sputtered. "Now, what—"

"Please, Mrs. Cobb! I think I saw Mandy Tate!"

"Mandy!" Heather gasped. "Why didn't you say so? Where was she? Was she all right?" Now Heather dragged Nellie into the office and closed the door. "Tell me about this! Did you see her at the store? Are you sure it was Mandy?"

"I'm not sure." Nellie started to cry, trying to talk between the sobs. "She was in a truck. It was going by on the street, and it slowed down for a moment, and she looked at me out the window. Then the truck sped up again and drove away. A pickup truck, a red one."

"Did you get the license plate?" Heather asked.

"No," Nellie sniffled, "but Mr. Cobb went after the truck."

Heather looked at her with narrowed eyes. "What was Justin doing here? Nellie, if you're making this up . . ."

Nellie looked up at her, her large dark eyes drowned in tears. "Oh, no, Mrs. Cobb, I wouldn't do that! Mr. Cobb was coming down the street on a bicycle, and I told him I'd seen Mandy, and he went off following the truck!"

Heather sat down at her desk. Her mind was spinning. Nellie said she had seen Justin on a bicycle—she wouldn't make that up, since she didn't even know that Justin loved racing bicycles. But the rest of the story seemed so crazy that she couldn't begin to believe it.

"All right, Nellie," she said in a voice that she hoped sounded more calm on the outside than she felt on the inside, "go and get the juice off the sidewalk, or wherever it is, and then go help Tina with story hour. I'll see what I can find out about your mysterious red truck."

As soon as Nellie had left the room, Heather reached

for the phone. The first call she made was to Manning's
Auto Sales. One of the other salesmen answered. "No," he
said, "now that you mention it, Heather, I haven't seen
Justin anywhere. He usually goes out for lunch with
Dave and me, but today he took off in his car, I think.
Lunch hour is over, and he'd better get himself back here
before the Old Man realizes he's missing!"

Heather asked the salesman to have Justin call her as
soon as he got back to work and hung up. Justin *knew*
that Mr. Manning would be furious if he was late getting
back from lunch. But if Nellie had set him to following
some pickup truck all over the city . . .

She had to find out for sure. She dialed Mrs.
Grasso's number.

"Oh, Heather," Mrs. Grasso said, "Justin picked me up
today and we went to see those families again. Mrs.
Ripley said she'd sent her daughter to the day care center
today, but you must know that already. And the
Hoffmans didn't come to the door. But wait until you
hear about the Scarpellis! They—"

"Mrs. Grasso, please!" Heather cut in. "What did Justin
do after he brought you back home?"

"Well, I assume he went back to work, didn't he?"

"Mrs. Grasso, would you please go look out your back
window and see if our car is still parked out in the alley?"

Mrs. Grasso put down the phone, and Heather could
hear her wheezing across the kitchen floor. A moment
later she was back to report, "Yes, the car is still there.
That's odd. I'm sure I heard him come down the stairs
just a few minutes after he dropped me off."

"I think he took his bicycle back to work," Heather said.
"He probably forgot that he'll have to pick me up. I'll look
pretty funny in my condition, riding on the handlebars."
Heather gave a little laugh for Mrs. Grasso's sake.

Then she called the police.

While she was waiting for them to arrive, she realized that she really ought to call Mrs. Tate. The poor woman called several times a day, and time after time Heather had to tell her that there was nothing new to report. Now there *was* news of Mandy—if Nellie was telling the truth—but Heather felt as if she didn't have the strength to talk to her. She'd become hysterical at the thought of Mandy riding around the city in a red truck.

Perhaps she should let the police call Mrs. Tate. It was their job, wasn't it?

Heather walked into the main room of the day care center and looked out the front window to see if there was any sign of the police. Nellie was out on the sidewalk with a bunch of paper towels, cleaning up the spilled juice. Wasn't it bad enough that food kept disappearing without Nellie smearing it all over the sidewalk?

Across the street something was moving—there was someone in the phone booth on the opposite sidewalk. She circled her face with her hands and pressed them against the window, straining to see against the glare from outside. The person waved at her.

Oh, she thought, *could it be Justin?* He called her sometimes from that phone booth, just to be funny. Not that anything could be funny these past few days, but—

Then she saw the person's head outlined against the wall behind it. There was only one head of hair like that in the world: Hugo.

She glanced around to be sure that Tina had the children all happy with the story hour, then opened the front door and stepped out onto the sidewalk. "That's good enough, Nellie," she said. "Go inside now and help Tina."

"Yes, Mrs. Cobb." Nellie gathered up the sticky paper towels and scurried into the building.

Heather waddled across the street and pulled open the door to the phone booth. "Hugo, what on earth are you doing here?" she demanded.

"Justin said I should follow Nellie. That was her hunkered down in front of the door, right? I'm just keeping an eye on her."

"Well," Heather said, shaking her head, "she doesn't get off work until 5:00, so you've got almost four hours to wait until she comes out again." Suddenly she looked up sharply at Hugo. "Wait a minute! How long have you been here? Did you see Justin?"

Hugo looked confused for a moment, as if he couldn't figure out which question to answer first. He took them in order. "I've been here for just a few minutes. I got into position just as Nellie came out the front door over there. And, um, yes, I did see Justin."

"Was he following a red pickup truck on his bicycle?"

Hugo looked even more puzzled. "He was in his car. I mean your car. I mean, the car that you two have. Only you weren't in it. Mrs. Grasso was in it. They were just coming back to your apartment building."

"Then what happened?" Heather asked.

"What happened? Well, nothing really happened." Hugo spread his hands wide, or as wide as he could get them inside the narrow phone booth. "He went inside the apartment building, and I started walking over here."

It figured. The one thing she really wanted to know, and Hugo had missed it. "You've been very helpful, Hugo," she said. "Keep up the good work."

Hugo beamed. "Right!" he said. "I'll bet you ladies will feel better knowing there's a man out here on guard!"

"That's fine, Hugo," Heather said. Then she turned and made her way back across the street to the familiar front door. As she looked at the children in their tiny chairs, she thought that it *would* be nice to have a man about.

She went back into her office, took a deep breath, and called Mrs. Tate. After that, she dug in her desk for the card with the number of the trucking firm that Henry Tate worked for.

*   *   *

At first things happened so fast that Justin, still recovering from the blow when his chin connected with his handlebar, didn't have time to think.

A short time later, after Hoffman and Mack had tied him thoroughly to a chair and left the garage, he had plenty of time to think.

He thought about Nellie, sending him off to fall into Hoffman's trap.

He thought about Heather, running her day care center, unaware that her husband was tied to a chair in an old garage a few blocks away.

He even thought about Old Man Manning having a fit when Justin didn't come back at the end of his lunch hour. He had to admit that Manning's showroom didn't seem quite so much like a prison compared to his present situation.

The chair he was tied to was squeezed between the back wall of the garage and the hood of the pickup truck. Justin strained to see as much of his surroundings as he could manage. The hood of the truck loomed over him on his right side. He could smell the hot engine and hear the tiny *pings* as the metal cooled down. His right elbow was crammed up against the truck's bumper, which was dirty and somewhat cool.

His left elbow was pressed against the wall of the garage, which consisted of old, unpainted wood with the points of the nails coming through from outside. One nail had already caught on the sleeve of his jacket as he squirmed in the chair.

There wasn't much in back of him, he assumed. But in front of him, packed in tightly from the truck over to the opposite wall, was the most incredible collection of stuff Justin had even seen.

It was all new stuff, as far as he could tell. Television sets of all sizes, radios, a snowmobile, several bicycles, microwave ovens, tires, and something that he finally recognized as a dishwasher looking very naked with no sides or countertop. It was as if the Hoffmans were getting ready for a huge garage sale, except that everything was brand new.

The stuff must have come from the boxes that were being flattened out in the alley. The boxes that Hoffman was afraid would give them away.

So that must mean the stuff was stolen. And Hoffman and Mack thought he had come here to catch them with the goods.

Boy, he'd sure done Mandy Tate a lot of good, if she ever had been in the truck, which now he rather doubted. Nellie had sure set him up.

But why? What was in it for Nellie to get him tied up in a garage?

He hoped it wouldn't be very long before he found out what was going on. His hands were tied behind him with a rope that also passed around his waist, through the legs of the chair, and around his ankles. The insides of his elbows were pulled tight against the back of the chair, and the rope was cutting off his circulation. Mack had also stuffed a rag—none too clean—into his mouth and put tape across the lower half of his face. The tape pulled on his skin, and if he thought about the rag in his mouth, he felt as if he was going to gag.

Time crawled by. In the distance, he could hear cars passing by on the street like any normal afternoon. Once a car drove slowly down the alley, its engine echoing loudly between the buildings packed closely on either side. He couldn't figure out why Mack had bothered gagging him. No one would ever hear him in this quiet, lonely spot in the middle of the noisy city.

Suddenly he heard a door slam somewhere behind him—the back door of the brick apartment building, he thought, judging by the direction. Footsteps crunched heavily in the gravel, coming rapidly nearer. Justin's stomach lurched. Whatever was next, he was going to find it out soon.

Then the door shut again, more quietly this time, and another set of footsteps came after the first—light footsteps, as if someone were running. "Ken," a woman's voice called. "Ken, wait a minute!"

"What do you want now?" snapped a voice that Justin recognized as Hoffman's. "Haven't you made enough trouble?"

"Ken, what are you going to do with him? You aren't going to—to *kill* him or anything, are you?" the woman asked.

There was a silence. Justin's heart was hammering so loudly that he could hardly hear the answer when it came.

"I don't know," Hoffman said at last. "Mack says we've got to get rid of him. Lord, I never figured on this happening! You know I don't want to, Eve, but maybe Mack's right. Maybe we've got to kill him."

CHAPTER 7

At Ken Hoffman's words, Justin felt his blood run cold.

He had always thought that was just an expression. But that was exactly what it felt like. Icy cold shot through every inch of his body, stabbing knives of cold in his guts and icy little prickles all over his skin. The outside world disappeared, and there was nothing but him, the chair, the rope that held him to it, and Ken Hoffman's words: *Maybe we've got to kill him.*

This couldn't be happening! Not to him! Heather was due to have her baby soon! He was going to be a father!

He forced himself to take a breath and another one. The world outside slowly returned and with it the voices outside.

"I'm pretty sure he's the same guy who knocked on our door upstairs a couple of hours ago," Hoffman was saying. "It was dark in the stairwell, but I got a look at

him as he was going out the front door. I don't think he's
a cop, but I just can't figure out who he is, or how he got
onto us!"

"You think it's got something to do with Mandy?" his
wife asked.

Mandy! Justin struggled to turn in the chair so that he
could hear better. So Mandy *was* here! Suddenly there
was more to think about than how much longer he was
going to live.

"What else could it be?" the man asked angrily.
"Everything was going just fine until Lisa brought that
Mandy kid home with her the other day. You'd think
she'd have more sense than to do something like that!"

"Come on, dear, Lisa's just a kid! Mandy followed
them home when she went to pick up Kyle and Rory,
and Lisa didn't even notice the poor little thing until
they were all the way back here. Besides, Lisa doesn't
know what kind of business you and Mack and the other
boys are running back here!"

"Well, *you* know what kind of business we're running!
And it's been a darned good business too! I haven't heard
you complaining when the money comes in! Why the
heck you didn't have the sense to take that kid right back
to that day care center just as soon as you got home—"

"I did take her back!" the woman snapped. "But when I
got there, there was a police cruiser parked right out
front! I knew the police were probably there because
they'd lost a child, but I was afraid to go in and have
some cop asking a bunch of questions about our family."

"I know," the man admitted. "I tried to take her back
today myself. I was just going to drop her off at the door
and take off, but one of the women who works there
spotted the kid and started hollering. I lost my nerve and
got out of there."

There was a pause. Then the man's voice came, angry again: "This is ridiculous! I'm going to take that kid and just dump her someplace—give her a push and tell her to start walking! I'm telling you, Eve, she'd be all right. Someone would pick her up and get her to where she belongs."

"No, Ken, there's no telling who'd pick her up, or if she'd get hit by a car! We're just not that kind of people! At least, we weren't up until now!"

The woman's voice had begun to shake, as if she was trying not to cry. "Oh, Ken, I'm beginning to wish you'd never got started in this—this whatever-you-call-it *business* of yours. It's ruining our family! The men are always here, in our way. We can never have a normal evening at home like other families, with kids doing homework or maybe watching a little television together—and I'm so *afraid* all the time! Every little knock on the door or car driving down the alley, and we're in a panic."

"Now, Eve, everything is going to be all right."

"Ken, I'm so afraid you'll get caught and get sent away!" The woman was crying now, Justin knew, because her voice was becoming ragged. "The children need you. I need you! And now *this*—you've got some guy tied up in the garage, and you're thinking of *killing* him!"

"Eve! Hush! Everyone can hear you out here! Get yourself inside the apartment *now*!"

Footsteps crunched in the gravel, and the voices faded away until they were finally ended by the slam of a door.

Justin felt exhausted. He let himself sag against the back of the chair, head drooping. If only Nellie hadn't been by the front door when Hoffman tried to bring Mandy back to the day care center! Mandy would have just waltzed in the front door. Everyone would have cried and hugged her for a while, and then life would have gone back to normal.

And he wouldn't be tied to a chair in a garage in an alley, waiting for people who were even more stupid than he was—if that was possible—to make up their minds about what to do with him.

His stomach growled, reminding him that his lunch hour had come and gone with no lunch. He was beginning to feel chilled through, especially his hands and feet where the ropes cut off the circulation. The tape across the lower part of his face was prickling against his skin.

He closed his eyes and lolled against the ropes in total misery. How long were they going to leave him here while they debated his fate in a nice, warm kitchen upstairs? He wished they would hurry up with whatever they decided and get it over with!

Then he began to get angry. Angry at Hoffman, angry at Mack for catching him looking in the window, angry at himself for getting caught.

This whole situation was just too stupid! He had to figure out a way to get away!

He opened his eyes. The first thing he needed to do was learn everything he could about where he was. He began a methodical search of the garage. He examined the back wall, board by board, as far as he could see to his left. Its only feature was a single spot of light from a window somewhere high up behind him, which must be mostly covered like the window he had looked through. His eyes checked through all the goods in front of him, every microwave and lawnmower and bicycle. If there was a pattern to what Hoffman's "business" brought in, Justin couldn't see it.

He gazed at every inch of the Dodge Ram's hood shoved up against his right arm until he had memorized every dent and scratch. He looked up at the inside of the roof, which was hung with dusty spiderwebs, then craned his neck to look at the floor around his feet and under the truck.

He wasn't sure what he was looking for, but he knew it when he spotted it. Lying on the floor in front of the right tire of the truck was a scrap of metal, a flat triangle shape, just a few inches on a side. It looked as if it might have been left over from some long-ago repair to a car or truck. If the edges were sharp, he might be able to use it like a knife to defend himself or even to cut the rope.

Was there any way he could reach it? He wriggled against the ropes until the sweat trickled down his forehead, but the ropes held fast. He threw himself forward, trying to hitch the chair forward along the floor until the nail points in the wall dug into his left arm. But the chair was wedged securely between the wall and the bumper of the truck. He wasn't going anywhere.

His head bowed low in exhaustion. *Have to rest*, he told himself. *Have to think.*

Have to wait.

There wasn't any other option.

Time passed.

Bit by bit, the sound of traffic increased on the surrounding streets: rush hour. People going home. The spot of light moved slowly up and across the wall. It must be late in the afternoon—it sure took these people a long time to think things through.

A single car came down the alley. It stopped, the engine died, and a moment later a door opened and closed. Justin threw himself against the ropes and cried out, but all he could manage was an inhuman gurgle. *This is what the gag is for*, he realized. There were footsteps, muffled in the soft dirt beyond the garage, and then a distant door slammed shut, leaving behind a small echo like a faraway gunshot.

Suddenly there were more footsteps, crunching heavily in the gravel, coming toward him. Beyond the truck, the overhead door rolled partway up on its tracks, just far enough to admit a person bent over. Then it dropped again with a rattling crash. And now there was the smell of food.

Justin's stomach lurched. Even before the person had walked to him along the far side of the truck, Justin could tell that the plate held freshly fried potatoes and some kind of meat. It smelled wonderful.

The plate rounded the cab of the truck, and behind it came Mack.

His shirtsleeves were rolled up to the elbows, revealing a series of homemade tattoos that looked as if they'd been created with a ballpoint pen. A cigarette dangled from his lips, and his chin was covered with two or three days' worth of stubble. He planted his feet in their heavy boots directly in front of Justin and glared down at him. "I don't know why they're bothering with this food," he said. "It's not like you're going to have time to starve to death out here."

Justin tried not to look at the plate. He tried to look Mack right in the eye, as if he didn't really mind being tied up in a chair with a filthy gag in his mouth.

Mack stared at him for a moment, probably trying to figure out how to get the meal into him without removing the gag. Then his hand snaked out, grabbed one end of the tape, and ripped it off Justin's face.

Justin's head snapped back at the shock of pain, and his eyes smarted with tears. He blinked his eyes quickly to clear them, and then, as coolly as he could manage, pushed the gag out of his mouth with his tongue. He sat looking up at Mack and waited.

Mack stuck a fork into the plateful of food and shoved it, mounded with buttery bits of potato, toward Justin's

mouth. Suddenly ashamed at having to be fed, Justin
didn't get his mouth open at the right moment, and most
of the potatoes slid down the front of his bicycle jacket.
Mack snorted with laughter, took another drag on the
cigarette, and rammed the fork into the food again. This
time the potatoes tumbled from the fork before he got
them even halfway to Justin's mouth. Justin felt them
plop against his knees on their way to the floor.

"This is crazy!" Mack snarled. "If she wants you fed, *she*
can do it!" He set the plate on the hood of the truck and
stamped away. "If I hear one word out of you, one tiny
little peep," he called from the doorway, "I'll come in here
and blow your head off." The overhead door rattled up
and then slammed down.

Justin was alone with the aroma of potatoes and meat.

He licked his lips, savoring the taste of the few bits
that had hit his mouth. He gazed at the plate where it
sat on the Dodge's hood and imagined it picking itself up
and hovering in the air in front of him. He tried to will
the fork to levitate and stab itself into that meat and
bring it over—

Behind his right shoulder, the overhead door lifted
again, more slowly, and stayed partway up. The footsteps
that came in, tentatively, as if on tiptoe, were the
woman's, he guessed.

Eve Hoffman walked along the far side of the truck as if
she was coming up onto the stage for graduation. She
stopped just out of sight and peeked at him around the cab.

"Hello," Justin said quickly. "I'm Justin Cobb, and I'm
the husband of Heather Cobb, the director of the Little
Friends Day Care Center. I only came looking for Mandy,
not for anything else."

The woman's eyes grew wide with fear, and her finger
shot up in front of her lips. "Mack told me not to talk to

you," she said in the tiniest whisper.

She picked up the plate in one hand and the fork in the other. Then she stepped forward until she was knee to knee with Justin. The fork slipped into the mound of potatoes, lifted up just the right amount, and came toward him at an even speed. In the next instant he had a mouthful of slightly cooled potatoes, and they were delicious. *Practice*, he thought. *She's had lots of practice in feeding kids.*

The woman carefully avoided looking into his eyes, but the food kept coming, forkful by forkful, with just the right amount of time in between for him to chew, until the plate was almost empty.

Suddenly a scream echoed into the garage from the direction of the apartment building, a child's scream of outrage and pain. It cut off sharply as the child ran out of breath. Eve Hoffman's head lifted as she listened. As if her body was acting on its own, she put the plate back down on the hood and moved swiftly away alongside the truck. A moment later Justin heard her feet pattering through the gravel, just as the scream sounded again, rising into a shriek.

Justin cranked his head around over his shoulder as far as it would go, trying to see out the partially opened door. Suddenly, although he had heard no sound, he was aware of a presence by his knees.

Standing in front of him, gazing up at him steadily with large, round, calm eyes was a little girl in purple pants rolled up at the ankles and a pink sweater that was also too big for her. Her face was dirty, as if she'd been eating, but her hair was neatly combed. She looked up at him as if seeing a strange man tied into a chair was the most natural thing in the world.

Even before she spoke to him, he knew exactly what she was going to say. "My name is Mandy Tate. What's your name?"

CHAPTER
8

Heather had reached Mrs. Tate at her apartment and Mr. Tate at his job. But they arrived at the day care center together just a few minutes after the police. Mrs. Tate must have taken care of being hysterical in the car on the way over, because she seemed nervous but under control as she came in the front door. Henry Tate loomed right behind her.

Heather ushered everyone into her office. Then she called in Nellie and closed the door. "Okay, Nellie," she said, "tell us what you saw."

"You sent me to the store," Nellie said to the floor. "I was just coming back—"

"Could you speak up, miss?" one of the policemen asked, his notebook at the ready.

The whites of Nellie's eyes gleamed as she glanced toward the policeman. Then she straightened herself up in her chair and forced herself to face him directly.

What's going on in her head? Heather wondered. *Is she making this up as she goes along?*

"I was coming back from the store," Nellie began again, "and just as I got to the front door, a pickup truck went by, and I saw Mandy looking at me through the window."

Next to Heather, Mrs. Tate let out a long breath, almost a sob, and laid her hand on her husband's arm. After an instant's hesitation, Heather saw Mr. Tate put his own big hand over his wife's little one.

"Can you describe the truck?" the policeman asked. "Did you see who was driving it?"

"No, I was just looking at Mandy," Nellie said. "I didn't see the driver or the license plate. All I can tell you is that it was red. And I think it had a load of stuff in the back. Mr. Cobb was just coming by on a bicycle, and when I told him I'd seen Mandy, he went after the truck."

The policeman's pen stopped in the middle of the notebook page. "On a bicycle?"

"Yes, my husband has a racing bicycle, which he sometimes uses while he's on his lunch hour," Heather explained. "He used to be a bicycle messenger, and in city traffic he would have no difficulty keeping up with a loaded pickup truck. I am sure," she said, filling her voice with steady confidence for the sake of the Tates, "that he will be able to follow the truck to its destination. We should hear from him at any moment."

Oh, Justin, she thought, *oh, please call us soon and tell us Mandy is all right.*

*   *   *

Justin stared at the child standing in front of him. The child stared back, unblinking, her face serene and untroubled, waiting for him to speak.

"My name is Justin Cobb," he said. "I'm very pleased to meet you, Mandy."

"I've seen you before," Mandy said. "You come to the day care sometimes. Is Mrs. Cobb your mother?"

Justin smiled. "She's my wife," he said. "She misses you, you know. Everyone at the day care center misses you."

Mandy looked serious. "I know. I wish Auntie Eve would take me and Rory and Kyle to day care. We have to go to Grandma Hoffman's. She's nice, but she doesn't have so many toys."

"Well, Mandy, how come you went home with the Hoffmans instead of waiting for your mama to pick you up?"

Mandy cocked her head to one side as if she wanted to see what he looked like from a different angle. "Rory and Kyle have sisters." She counted them off on her fingers: "They have Lisa and Rachel. And Auntie Eve and Uncle Ken are nice. They live together in the same apartment, and they don't fight all the time." The corners of her mouth drooped. "My daddy doesn't come home any more. Mommy says he lives in his truck."

With every word out of the child's mouth, Justin's mind was racing—he had to get himself and Mandy out of there before someone came back. He said carefully, "How are you at untying knots? Can you untie me?"

Mandy looked at him solemnly and asked, "Did Uncle Ken put those ropes around you?"

"Um, yes, he did. We were playing a game, and—"

"I can't touch anything that belongs to Uncle Ken. He said."

"All right," Justin said. So far, the child had not been in any danger from the Hoffmans, and he certainly wanted to keep it that way. "Well, there's something else you could do for me. See that little piece of metal on the floor, right by the tire of the truck? That's mine, but I dropped it, and now I can't pick it up. Mr. Hoffman wouldn't like it on the floor, because it might hurt his truck. Can you pick it up and give it to me?"

Mandy nodded and bent down to reach for the bit of metal. "Careful, it's sharp," Justin said. "Can you reach around me and put it in my hand?"

The little girl had to crouch under the truck's bumper to reach his hand. Her tiny fingers were cool and soft as she placed the piece of metal into his palm. He folded his thumb over it, wondering if that would hide it.

She straightened up and leaned against the bumper, waiting to see what he would do next.

Justin strained his ears, listening for returning footsteps. Everything seemed to be quiet out in the alley. Maybe there were so many kids in that apartment that no one had noticed that Mandy was missing. "Mandy, Mrs. Cobb says you know your letters. Can you write them?" Mandy nodded her head up and down until her hair bounced. "Will you show me?"

"I don't have a pencil," Mandy pointed out.

"You can write with your finger on the truck, right here by my elbow, where it's dusty. Can you make an H?"

"That's two standing-up lines with a line in the middle," Mandy said.

"That's right. Can you make one right there for me?"

Mandy obliged, running her fingertip along the red paint until she had created a somewhat crooked capital H.

"How about an O? Can you make an O next to the H? That's right. Can you make an F? Yes, that's a good F. I like F's, so could you make another one right next to it? Now how about an M, that's right, and an A, and an N."

Mandy looked at her N. "What should I make next?"

"That's enough. Mrs. Cobb was right, you really do know your letters."

Outside, heavy footsteps crunched across the gravel.

"Mandy!" Justin whispered. But the child had already ducked under the bumper and crawled around the back of his chair. As the footsteps came along the side of the truck, she melted away on the other side. By the time Mack appeared around the cab with a fresh piece of tape in his hand, Mandy was simply gone.

Mack picked up the gag. He was standing where Mandy had been standing, his left leg almost brushing the spidery letters she had scrawled in the dust. "Hey," Justin said, to get him to look away, "what about my supper?"

Mack glanced at the plate sitting on the hood of the truck and smirked. "It'd be cold by now anyway," he said and shoved the gag into Justin's mouth. He slapped the tape across Justin's face, stomped away alongside the truck, and yanked the overhead door down with a crash.

Immediately, the fingers of Justin's right hand delicately retrieved the little piece of metal from his left palm, touched it carefully all the way around to find the sharpest edge, and began to rub it against the rough fibers of the rope that bound his wrists.

Justin sat in the darkening garage, trying not to think about the almost impossible thickness of the rope compared with this piece of metal which was his only hope. He tried not to think about the gag, or the fact that he couldn't feel his feet, or how Heather must be worrying.

Instead, as his fingers worked, he thought about little Mandy. She didn't seem to be afraid of anything. But when Mack came in, it hadn't taken her a moment to disappear, like a four-year-old ghost.

For that kid, he thought, *making a getaway from the day care center must have been a piece of cake.*

*   *   *

Heather's office at the day care center began to seem very small for the five people who were squeezed into it waiting for the phone to ring.

"I'm sure Justin will call any moment," Heather said every few minutes. "He must have followed that truck a long way, and then he's got to find a telephone—"

Henry Tate squirmed in his chair, obviously impatient to *do* something—*anything*. Mrs. Tate sat with her hands folded in her lap and her eyes closed. Sometimes it seemed as if she had stopped breathing.

Heather flipped through the paperwork on her desk, but the words and figures on the food orders just danced in front of her eyes, meaningless. She could feel the other people in the office, feel them thinking about Mandy, feel them waiting.

How did I get into this? Heather wondered. *Everything depends on what Nellie said she saw. What if Nellie made it all up? What if we're waiting for nothing?*

Eventually the police departed, telling Heather to call them as soon as she heard from Justin. Heather left the Tates on guard over the telephone and went to help Tina and Nellie get the children ready to go home. As the mothers and fathers and older sisters and brothers arrived, Heather scanned each face. She knew them all.

She told Nellie that she could leave as usual at 5:00. As Nellie put on her coat and quietly pushed open the front door, Heather hurried to the front window.

Nellie stopped for a moment to pull her braid out from under her coat collar and let it swing free down her back, then walked quietly away up the sidewalk. There was no movement in the phone booth. *Oh, well*, Heather told herself, *it doesn't matter.*

She picked up the last few bits of train track and began to turn away from the window. Just then a dark shape slipped out of the phone booth, sketched her a quick wave, and hurried down the other side of the street in the same direction that Nellie had taken.

Heather smiled to herself. If nothing else, Hugo was faithful. He must have known it was her standing in the window by her fat-lady outline, and he recognized Nellie as she came out the door. He *might* even notice if Nellie did something strange. At least that was something.

Now she had to talk the Tates into going home.

*   *   *

The silence in the garage was broken abruptly by the rattle of the overhead door.

Quickly Justin tucked the piece of metal back into his palm. As footsteps came up behind him, his heart hammered. He couldn't help cringing back into the chair as the man came closer. His ears became antennae, listening for the tiny click of a gun being cocked. Or would they hit him first? His head felt naked, exposed, waiting for the gun butt to smash down on him.

Nothing happened. Nothing but the perfectly normal sound of the truck door opening, then closing. The engine roared into life under his right ear. Justin had an instant to imagine what it would be like to be crushed between the truck's bumper and the nail points on the back wall. Then the truck backed out of the garage.

The empty space where the truck had been seemed like a huge cavern. Justin looked toward the door just in time to see Mack pulling the garage door shut again. The truck's passenger door slammed shut, and the truck pulled away and echoed down the alley.

It was getting very dark in the garage. And cold. His hands were growing numb, making it harder and harder to keep the piece of metal lined up with the heartbreakingly tiny groove that had finally begun to wear in the rope.

Justin wondered if his hands would work any more when he got out of this. *If* he got out of this.

Suddenly the alley was full of the sound of the truck again. No, several trucks. Various doors slammed, and men's voices sounded here and there outside, muffled by the distance. Coming closer.

The overhead door rattled up, and the Dodge pulled in, closer, closer, until Justin was holding his breath, watching the metallic gleam of the big bumper pushing toward him. It stopped a foot from his elbow. Hoffman and Mack got out and went to join the other men, whom Justin could see peering in at him in the darkness. For safety's sake, he pushed his precious piece of metal up inside the cuff of his bicycle jacket.

Outside, the murmur of voices grew. Then a man's voice said clearly, "I want out, Hoffman. I'm willing to take the risks for moving around a few bits of stolen property. The big department stores won't miss a microwave oven here and there. But I never signed on for kidnapping. And I'm not going to be part of killing anyone."

Other voices were raised in agreement. "I'm out too, Hoffman," another man said. "I've done what I agreed to do. Give me my cut now, and I'm out of here."

"Wait a minute, boys," Hoffman's voice said. "Let's not be hasty. Mack and I will figure something out. We'll take care of this guy, and then everything'll be right back the way it was. Come on, you boys are making good money. This business is too good to give up."

"I've got a family, Hoffman. I want to watch my kids grow up, not read about them in letters while I'm doing twenty or thirty years in jail. Give me my cut now, and I'm gone." There was a hard edge to the man's voice, an unspoken threat that said *or else*—

"That's right," another voice said. "Let's settle up now."

"Me, too. I want my cut *now*, Hoffman, and then you can forget you ever met me," said a third voice.

"Okay," Hoffman said. "But you're going to be missing out on a lot of gravy. Here's yours, Tony. Gene. Red."

Hoffman must have been doling out large bills from his pocket as he spoke. Without any further talk, doors slammed, engines gunned, and the trucks roared away.

Hoffman stepped into the garage and waited while Mack pulled the overhead door down and flicked on a light. Then they both walked alongside the truck and stared down at Justin.

Mack leaned against the bumper just behind Justin's shoulder, ready for action like a cat. Justin could smell the smoke from his cigarette. "This is all *your* fault!" he snarled.

Hoffman seemed to be too angry to speak. His head swiveled away from Justin, toward the front of the truck. Suddenly he stiffened. "What's *that*?" he demanded. He was pointing at the letters Mandy had made in the dust.

Mack gawked at the word. "It says *Hoffman*!"

"I know what it says, you idiot! How did it get there? Haven't his hands been tied the whole time?"

"Maybe it was one of the kids—"

"The kids know better than to come in here!"

"Then it's got to be him!" Mack said from behind Justin.

Hoffman nodded his head slightly.

The blow, when it came, was still absolutely unexpected. Justin's vision exploded in a burst of whirling bright lights and pain. Then all was dark.

CHAPTER 9

As Mrs. Grasso drove Heather home through dark streets lit by the glare of streetlamps and storefronts, Heather peered down each alley and side street.

She was hoping against hope to see someone approaching on a bicycle. But there were no bicycles, just the evening flow of traffic and a few people on foot, out for a walk or returning home late from work.

She thanked Mrs. Grasso for the ride and hauled her weary fat-lady self up the stairs. No one was home, she knew, because there was no crack of light under the door, no sound of Justin's favorite CD on the player. She paused for a long moment before unlocking the door and pushing it open.

The apartment seemed huge and empty, as if no one really lived there anymore. In the glare of the streetlamp outside the window, the furniture looked unfamiliar.

Heather shook herself, flicked on the light, and stepped into the apartment. She laid her bag on the kitchen counter as she always did and hung up her coat in the closet as she always did. She headed for the stove and turned on the heat under the kettle for a cup of tea.

The phone rang.

She snatched the receiver off the wall before it could ring a second time. "Hello? Hello?" she gasped.

"Mrs. Cobb?" asked a gruff voice. "Could I possibly speak with Mr. Cobb, if it wouldn't be *too* much trouble? This is Alton Manning of Manning's Luxury Auto Sales. I *think* I am Mr. Cobb's employer."

"Oh, Mr. Manning," Heather stuttered. "Yes, Justin—um—Justin was called away, he—um—he had a family emergency, and—"

"And no one could find time to call and let me know." Manning's voice sounded like rainwater running down a storm sewer. "Well, would you kindly give Mr. Cobb a message for me? He spent the morning with a gentleman who was interested in a black Jaguar. Tell him that the gentleman came back this afternoon and bought the Jaguar. The sale would have brought Mr. Cobb a very nice commission. But since Mr. Cobb was not with us, it became a nice commission for someone else. It was Dave Santino, I think, who clinched the sale."

"I'll tell him," Heather said, but Manning had already hung up. "Dirty old man!" she said into the dead phone.

As long as she had the receiver in her hand, she called Mrs. Tate as she had promised, to report that there was nothing to report. She could hear Henry Tate in the background, rumbling out questions, and she felt a stab of jealousy. *At least they seem to have each other*, she thought.

The kettle on the stove whistled and Heather went

about making herself a cup of tea. She couldn't even think about supper.

Out in the hallway, slow footsteps and a heavy wheezing announced Mrs. Grasso's creaking progress up the stairs. Heather opened the door just as Mrs. Grasso got ready to knock, and Clarence shot into the room and careened around, sniffing at things.

"I knew you'd be tired," Mrs. Grasso said, "maybe too tired to make yourself any supper, so I brought you some." She lugged a tray over to the kitchen table and began to set out dishes laden with enough food to feed herself, Heather, Justin, and Hugo too. She turned to face Heather, hands on hips. "You have to eat, ducky. If not for yourself, for the baby."

In the corner of the living room, the dog growled a tiny growl at a pair of Justin's shoes. "Shut up, Clarence!" Heather snapped. "Justin's not here to defend himself against your bad opinion of him!" Then, sighing, she went to the kitchen cabinet and took down a plate and a glass.

"What were you telling me on the telephone," Heather asked as she set the table, "about going with Justin at lunchtime to see those three families?"

"Well, Mrs. Ripley said she sent her little girl back to day care today, so she's off our list."

"Yes, I saw her today," Heather said.

"Then we went to see the Hoffmans," Mrs. Grasso went on, "and I think I heard someone moving around, but when I knocked, no one came to the door."

Heather shrugged. "Maybe they thought you were selling something."

"I don't know. But then we went to see the Scarpellis." Mrs. Grasso leaned forward and dropped her voice to a whisper. "And they had disappeared!"

"Disappeared?" Heather turned to look at her, the knives and forks still in her hand. "What do you mean, they'd disappeared?"

"Well, we got to their apartment building," Mrs. Grasso said, "and the apartment door was standing open. The place was empty. Absolutely stripped to the walls!"

"Wow!" Heather said. "Did you report this to anyone?"

"Well," Mrs. Grasso said, "I told *you*."

"Oh, yes." Heather rushed to the phone, still holding the knives and forks. "I've got to call the police and tell them about this!"

The policemen who had come to the day care center that afternoon had gone home for the day. The desk sergeant was less than impressed with the Scarpellis' disappearance. "People move," he said. "It's a free country."

"But this might be a clue to finding Mandy Tate, the little girl who's missing from the Little Friends Day Care Center!" Heather told him. "And now my husband is missing too! He left work at lunchtime, and there's been no word from him."

"Maybe he just needs some time to himself once in a while," the desk sergeant said in a bored voice. "Yes, yes, Mrs. Cobb, I'm writing it all down. I'll make a full report. Let us know if there are any developments. Good night, Mrs. Cobb."

Heather threw herself into her chair. "Well, *he* was a big help!" she said.

"We'll talk to the police again in the morning," Mrs. Grasso said, heaping her plate with linguine in clam sauce. "Now eat your supper."

"Aren't you going to have some?"

"Oh, I've already had mine. This is all for you!"

Heather bent sideways to pat Clarence, who was now sitting on her feet, yapping for attention. *How could I feel so completely squashed by Mrs. Grasso and her dog*, she asked herself, *and yet feel so completely alone?*

*   *   *

The apartment felt hollow in the morning without the sound of Justin humming in the shower and the smell of Justin's coffee as it gurgled through the coffeemaker. Heather couldn't help thinking, as she drove herself along the familiar streets to the day care center, that this might be her life from now on.

She felt a little better as the children started to arrive at the day care center, all fresh and clean and full of energy. She hurried to get out the fingerpaints and settle the first-comers down on the floor in front of huge sheets of brown paper.

Tina bustled in, called a quick greeting to Heather, and went right to work helping the children as they came in. "Don't you look nice in your brand-new sneakers this morning!" she exclaimed over one little boy. "And here comes my favorite redhead!" she called to another. "Good morning, Mrs. Sanchez! How's everyone at home? All through with that nasty cold that was going around? Good, good. Here, honey, let me help you with that mean old zipper!"

Heather couldn't help smiling at her cheerfulness. What a great help Tina was! Maybe she *could* manage the day care center while Heather was on maternity leave.

She turned back to the group with the fingerpaints and found Nellie hunkered down on the floor with the children, opening the little jars of paint for them. Heather stiffened. "Oh, Nellie! I didn't see you come in!"

"Good morning, Mrs. Cobb," Nellie said without looking up. She handed one child a jar of blue paint and picked up a jar of red. A little girl squatting next to her pointed to the large splotch of yellow that she had just smeared onto the paper. Nellie smiled, murmured something to the girl, and bent to roll up the child's sleeves away from the paint.

Heather turned and headed toward the kitchen. How did Nellie manage to sneak up in back of her like that? Why couldn't she say hello when she arrived, like Tina did? Like a normal person?

She pushed open the door to the kitchen and gasped. Just for an instant, a man's face appeared framed in the kitchen window. Then, as quickly as it had appeared, it was gone.

Should she call the police? The window and the back door were securely locked, but—

Then she heard a sound at the back door. A thump, a muffled knock. Her heart beat faster, and her mouth felt dry. Was the man trying to get in? She started to back out of the kitchen, her eyes darting from the back door to the door of her office. Or should she try to use the phone in the kitchen—

"Heather!" called a faint voice. "Heather, let me in!"

Cautiously, Heather stepped toward the back door, her eyes on the metal bolt. "Who is it?" she called.

"It's me, Hugo!"

Heather's breath burst out of her in relief. "Oh, Hugo," she said as she pulled back the bolt and Hugo fell into the room, "you really scared me!"

He looked more rumpled than ever, somehow, and his eyes were bloodshot. "I wanted to get you while you were alone in here." He stopped and looked around him. "Hey, this is a kitchen! Do you have anything to eat?"

Heather fixed him a peanut butter and jelly sandwich, noticing that there was only one more jar of peanut butter in the cupboard. Weren't there at least three jars yesterday after lunch? What was going on around here?

"So I followed Nellie home yesterday," Hugo mumbled through a mouthful of sandwich. "She lives all the way over on North 18th Street. Luckily she walked the whole way. I wasn't sure what I would do if she got on a bus."

"Mm-hmm," Heather murmured, looking in the other cupboards to see if the extra peanut butter had been put back in the wrong place.

"She went into her apartment building and up to the fifth floor. I was real quiet, following her on the stairs. There's a place where the hallway turns the corner, so I put myself there to watch who came in and out. Hey, this peanut butter is gluing my teeth together! A peanut butter and jelly sandwich needs a glass of milk!"

Heather fetched him a glass of milk. "So who came in and out?"

"There were three guys and a woman."

Heather's ears pricked up. "You mean, like a gang?"

Hugo chuckled and took a big swallow of milk. "Naw, like a family. I'd say two of the guys were her brothers, younger ones, and the other guy looked like he could be her father. And the woman was older, maybe her grandmother."

"So then what happened?" Heather asked.

"Well, they moved around a lot for a while, and I could smell their supper cooking." At that painful memory he shoved the rest of the sandwich into his mouth. "Then the TV was running, and then it got quiet."

"So you went home?"

"No, I stayed right there!" Hugo said. "I kind of curled up in the corner until I heard them moving around again in the morning."

"Hugo, you spent the whole night in the hallway?"

Hugo grinned proudly. "Yup! I didn't let Nellie out of my sight for a moment—well, her apartment, anyway. Then I followed while she walked her littlest brother to school, and then she came here. You know, she's kind of sweet. I like how she looks with that long braid of hers."

Heather let that comment pass. "Oh, Hugo, if anyone had caught you in that hallway, you could have been arrested!" She patted him on the arm. "I'll make you another sandwich, and then you'd better go home and get some sleep."

Just then the kitchen door swung open. Tina stood in the doorway, gawking at Hugo. "Heather," she said without taking her eyes off him, "the police are here to see you."

"Oh! Do they have news of—of Mandy?" Heather cried. "Quick, tell them to come in here! This," she added, nodding her head in Hugo's direction, "is an old friend of my husband's."

Tina tore her eyes off Hugo's wild-man hairdo and stepped back to admit a policewoman carrying a bundle.

"Mrs. Cobb, do you recognize these?" the policewoman asked. She unrolled the bundle and laid a suitcoat and a pair of shoes on the table.

Heather swayed and grasped the back of Hugo's chair for support. "Those are my husband's," she whispered. "I think he was wearing them when he went to work yesterday."

The policewoman nodded. "We found a credit card receipt in the pocket of the suitcoat," she said, "with his name on it."

Hugo slid out of his chair and put his arms around Heather. "Where did you find the clothes?" he asked.

"In a dumpster over on the west side," she said. "They were in the saddlebag of a busted-up racing bicycle."

CHAPTER 10

The first thing Justin became aware of was the terrible pain in his head.

He just lay there on his side, just concentrating on drawing in a breath and letting it out. The pain was so intense that it made him sick to his stomach.

Little by little, he realized that part of the sickness in his stomach was because he was moving, swaying and jiggling, starting and stopping, as if he were riding in a car.

And the reason he couldn't move was because he was tied.

And then he remembered.

He remembered being tied to the chair in the garage and the nod of Ken Hoffman's head. Mack must have hit him from behind.

But he wasn't tied to the chair anymore. He was lying on his side, with his ankles tied together and his hands tied behind his back. Something beneath him poked into his ribs. And there was that nasty swaying and stopping.

And he had the awful feeling he *was* in a car—in the trunk.

He fought through the pain in his head and forced his eyes open.

Darkness.

In the city even at night there is light—from streetlamps, storefronts, apartment windows.

In the trunk of a car, there is only darkness.

He lay still for a few long moments, wondering where they were taking him and what they would do with him when they got there. *You don't put someone in the trunk of a car*, he thought, *unless you intend to kill him.* His eyes drifted shut on the darkness. The car turned a corner, and he felt as if he were hanging upside down and the blood was piling up inside his skull.

Suddenly anger flared up inside him. *No, I'm not going to die! I want to live to see my child!* He struggled against the rope that tied his wrists, yanking his arms to see if he could create any slack. The rope held.

Then he remembered the piece of metal.

Was it still in his sleeve? Had they found it when they tied him? Gingerly, he poked his fingertips up into the cuff of his jacket.

The piece of metal was still there.

Let's hear it for bicycle jackets! he thought. But would he have time to cut through the rope before they reached their destination? He had worked on it forever in the garage without cutting through. If he had to start over . . . He bent his hand double to touch the rope where it passed between his wrists. Yes! He could feel the frayed edges where he had worked with the metal before! They hadn't untied and retied his wrists. He was halfway to freedom already!

If he didn't count the fact that he would still be locked in the trunk.

Well, the trunk wouldn't be locked forever. In the meantime he had work to do. He slid the piece of metal carefully out of his jacket cuff, pivoted it in his fingertips until it was lined up at exactly the same spot as before, and began to rub it back and forth on the rope.

It had been easier to cut through the stiff fibers before, back in the garage, when he was tied upright to the chair. Now his elbows banged into each other and interfered with the cutting motion of the metal. Every time the car went around a corner or hit a bump, he had to realign the metal with the tiny slot in the rope. The muscles in his arms and hands kept bunching up in cramps. The pain in his head and the churning of his stomach didn't help either, not to mention whatever was digging into his ribs.

He thought about Heather and worked until the sweat beaded on his forehead and his muscles jerked with the effort.

The car slowed and came to a stop. Justin's heart hammered—had they arrived at wherever they were going? Then the car lurched forward again. The piece of metal jerked in Justin's hand and sliced into his skin. *They must have stopped at a traffic light*, Justin thought, and went back to working the metal against the rope, ignoring the trickle of blood slippery under his fingertips. He didn't dare stop and check how far he had cut into the rope.

How far were they going? How long had he been unconscious? How many people were in the car? His mind raced with questions. And all the time, up and down, up and down, his fingers pushed and pulled at the piece of metal in a tiny sawing motion on the rope between his wrists until his hands were nothing but a series of knots and cramps.

He tried to work out a plan. The car would stop— somewhere. The trunk would be opened. And he would—do what? Against how many?

The only thing he would have going for him would be the moment of surprise. And that would be only a moment, and only once. He had to be ready.

The car lurched around one corner, then another, then rolled across bumpy ground and came to a stop. Over the sound of the engine, Justin could hear the sound of waves slapping against wood. The river! They were going to throw him in the river! With a new strength born of desperation, he ripped at the rope.

Suddenly, with a sharp jerk, the car pulled forward again. The piece of metal slipped out of Justin's fingers.

He scrabbled for it on the floor of the trunk, among the tools and other nameless bits and pieces he had been lying on. The car rolled forward, bouncing over ruts, and came to a stop.

With a sudden, awful silence, the engine died.

The blood thundered in Justin's ears. In despair, he gave one last mighty heave against the rope. This time it snapped, and the coils of rope slid away from his wrists like live snakes.

Quickly, he pulled his arms in front of him and dug at the rope around his ankles, trying to find the end, but his cramped fingers were too sore and stiff to feel the knots.

The car door on the driver's side opened, the car heaved as someone got out, and the door thunked shut again.

One person. But what if there are more in the car or somewhere nearby? Justin gripped the cut end of the rope, holding a length of it stretched taut between his hands a foot apart, and waited.

Footsteps crunched in the gravel alongside the car. A key snicked into the trunk's lock. The trunk lid lifted.

For an instant, Justin saw the man standing over him as

a dark bulk against the dim light of the sky. Then he burst up out of the trunk with a terrible roar.

As the man staggered back in surprise, Justin threw himself upon him with all his weight. He aimed the length of rope directly for the man's throat. They went down together hard in the dirt with Justin on top.

The man recovered quickly. He wrapped huge hands around Justin's face and pushed backward. But Justin pressed the length of rope against the man's throat and leaned into it with all his strength. He would fight to the end. He had no choice. He could not run.

The man gasped for breath and clawed at Justin's face. He rocked desperately from side to side, trying to throw Justin off. But Justin leaned and leaned against the rope. Then he drew his legs up, still bound together, and pressed one knee hard into the man's stomach.

The man let out an inhuman gurgle and clutched at his stomach, then fell back and lay still.

Justin slacked off on the rope, keeping it ready, but kept his knee pressed into the man's stomach. For the first time, he looked at the man's face.

Yes, it was Mack.

Mack was breathing in ragged gasps. Justin hurried to tie his wrists together with the loose end of the rope. The big man still looked entirely too powerful lying there with only his wrists tied, but the loose end of the rope that still bound his own ankles wouldn't be long enough to tie Mack's legs. If Justin could drag Mack's huge body into a bent position—which he doubted he'd be able to do anyway. *If only I hadn't taken off my necktie yesterday at noontime*, he thought wryly. In the end, he hauled Mack's arms up and tied them firmly to the bumper of the car.

He sat for a moment beside Mack's unconscious form, listening. No one else had jumped out of the car when he roared up from the trunk. No one had grabbed him when he choked the breath out of Mack. For the moment, he and Mack were alone with the car and the dark river sliding by.

As he breathed deeply of the night air, he rubbed his hands together, trying to get the blood flowing again into his fingers. His shoulders and arms ached, and his head still felt as if it was on fire. *I'll live*, he thought. He'd been through worse in his bicycle messenger days when he'd been hit by a car and woke up in the hospital. For now, he was content just to be alive and out of that trunk.

But sooner or later someone would miss Mack. He got to work on the knots that bound his ankles.

Even with the advantage of being upright and having his hands free, he couldn't get the knots to give up. In his struggles he had pulled the knots so tight that the rope had become a solid mass holding his feet tightly together.

This was ridiculous! He had managed to leave himself tied to Mack and to the car! What kind of freedom was this?

Then he realized that Mack's breathing had quieted. He glanced over at the still form lying under the car's bumper and realized that Mack's eyes were open.

Mack was looking at him.

Justin said nothing. Mack said nothing.

Justin pulled himself to his feet, and rooted around among the tools in the trunk, looking for something to cut the rope. He pulled out a jack, an ice scraper, and a sack of birdseed. *Birdseed? Whose car was this?* It was a big old Bonneville, probably belonged to Mack's mother. Even if she didn't mind her son using it to dump people into the river, she sure didn't stock it with rope-cutting tools.

There might be something in the glove compartment or under the seats of the car, but the front of the car might as well be a million miles away at the moment.

Justin was stuck with what he could find back here.

On the ground beside him, Mack stared up at him with deep, silent hatred.

Justin smiled grimly to himself, then took the blanket and laid it over the upper half of Mack's body. It made a sort of tent where Mack's arms were tied to the bumper. Mack didn't try to shake the blanket off. Perhaps he was glad for the warmth in the cool night air.

Then Justin knelt down beside Mack and went through his pockets. Mack didn't move, but Justin heard his teeth grinding together in fury and hoped it meant he was about to find a knife.

His anger was wasted. No knife. Well, Justin knew one thing that would work on that rope—eventually. He pulled himself to his feet again and poked around in the trunk until he found his trusty piece of metal. Then he dropped himself down to a sitting position on the ground and set to work.

From this angle, he was able to put much more pressure on the rope and the fibers parted more quickly. But it was still a thick rope, and the metal's edges had become dull. He sawed away, aware of time passing, of night slowly turning toward morning.

Mack lay beside him, breathing quietly. Why didn't he struggle? Why didn't he try to get away? The longer he lay there without moving, the more nervous Justin became. What was Mack thinking about under that blanket? What was he planning?

Suddenly Justin couldn't stand it anymore. He lunged over and yanked the blanket off Mack's head.

Mack's eyes, deep wells of darkness, were fixed on Justin's face.

Justin shuddered, then controlled himself and spread the blanket over Mack's body, drawing it up under his arms and taking time to tuck it carefully under his sides. *If it's mind games you're playing*, he thought, *well, I can play too!*

He went back to work on the rope that twisted between his ankles as if it intended to remain a permanent part of his body. This was taking too long! Already the eastern sky was lightening.

Now he could see that the car was near the edge of some sort of rough parking lot. An old chain-link fence around it was broken through or bent right down to the ground in several places. In the distance were blocks of large wooden buildings that looked like warehouses, some of them standing open and empty, one just a burned-out shell. No one was about. It looked as if the whole area was seldom used any more, all in all a perfect place to dispose of a body.

Once the sky began to get light, the day came faster and faster until soon it was full daylight. It wouldn't be long before someone came looking for Mack. Justin had to get out of there!

He pulled himself up again and took the tire iron out of the jack. He jammed the iron into the mess of rope between his ankles, just under the groove he had cut with the piece of metal, and twisted.

The rope creaked—or was that his ankle bone? The hard metal rod of the tire iron crushed against his ankles while the rope tried to cut through his skin and bones— but still he pressed down on the iron. Something would have to give. He was betting his life on the rope.

With a dry pop, the rope snapped. The tire iron flew free, and Justin slammed down onto his knees. Gingerly he stood up, testing to see if anything was broken, if his feet would hold him up.

Nothing was. They did.

Okay. He looked around him, trying to figure out what to do next. He would have to untie Mack from the bumper and lift his huge bulk into the car somehow, then drive the car back into the city and find a police station.

Wait! A car was coming, the first car he'd heard all night long, somewhere beyond the warehouses. He stood looking toward the sound.

When it suddenly appeared on the narrow street that ran between two warehouses toward the parking lot, it wasn't a car. It was a pickup truck. A red Dodge Ram.

This was the moment Mack had been waiting for. He launched a mighty kick at Justin's stomach.

Justin saw the motion out of the corner of his eye and leapt back. The kick connected, but not squarely. Justin went over backward and the ground came up at him hard and knocked the wind out of him for an instant. He dragged himself to his feet again, gasping for breath, and wheeled around. The truck was already turning into the far end of the parking lot.

There was time to get into the Bonneville, but no time to untie a screaming, cursing Mack. Justin hesitated for a fraction of a second, but as long as he had any option, he wasn't going to drag Mack's body behind the car.

He circled the Bonneville, putting it between him and the truck, and dashed for a break in the chain-link fence.

CHAPTER 11

Heather stared at Justin's second-best brown suitcoat dangling from the policewoman's hand.

She remembered Justin picking it out of the closet yesterday morning and sliding his arms into the sleeves. The way he settled the coat on his shoulders, checked the knot in his tie, and then turned to her for inspection with that funny little crooked smile that said *How do I look?*

She took the coat from the officer's hand and stroked it as if it had been a cat. She felt a lump and reached into the pocket to pull out his neatly rolled tie.

It seemed like a message from Justin. She could imagine so clearly his long fingers moving with their usual precision to roll the tie, smoothing the fabric as he went and then tucking it into the pocket before shrugging out of the coat.

The room began to spin around her. Hugo's arms

folded around her, holding her up, guiding her into a chair. She clutched the coat to her, as if she were afraid that someone was going to snatch it away from her. Mandy had disappeared without a trace. At least there was this much left of Justin.

"Mrs. Cobb," a second policeman said gently, "I'm Officer Prentiss, and I need to ask you some questions. When was the last time you saw your husband?"

"When he dropped me off here for work yesterday morning," Heather whispered. Could it be only yesterday? It felt like years ago.

"Now, yesterday you told us that he had been seen near here on a bicycle, in pursuit of a red pickup truck," the policeman went on, consulting his notebook. "He was seen by an employee of yours, Nellie Ramirez." He looked up at Heather, and she nodded. "You called the police station last night about two families you thought might be connected with the disappearance of Mandy Tate."

At least the desk sergeant last night had been paying attention, Heather thought. She made an effort to pull herself together, but her voice came out in a croak: "Yes, the Scarpellis—"

Echoing suddenly through the kitchen like a fire alarm, the telephone rang.

Justin! It must be Justin! Heather jumped up so fast that the blood drained out of her head and the room darkened around the edges of her vision. She dropped back into the chair, then struggled to rise again against Hugo's restraining hands on her shoulders. "The telephone—" she whimpered.

The phone stopped ringing. Tina's voice called, "Nellie, it's for you!"

"No, no," Heather cried, "Justin—"

"Sshh," Hugo comforted her. "Sshh. Don't worry. We'll find Justin. And I'll bet when we find Justin, he'll have Mandy with him. You'll see." Hugo's voice was soft. It rose and fell like a mother singing to a baby. "You'll see, Heather, he'll be all right, you'll see."

If it had been anyone but Hugo, Heather might have been able to believe him.

The policeman sat down at the table with Heather to get more information about the Hoffmans and the Scarpellis for his little notebook. Hugo lost interest and wandered out into the main room, then came bounding through the door again and thumped into the policeman just as he was getting up. "We'll do some checking on those families, Mrs. Cobb," the policeman said as he walked out into the main room to collect his partner.

"Heather!" Hugo said, holding the door open. "Nellie has something to tell you! Nellie, tell her about the phone call!"

Nellie stood in the doorway and stared at the floor as if there were something interesting written on the grubby linoleum tiles. "The Scarpellis called," she murmured.

Heather's chair fell backwards to the floor with a sharp clatter. "Why didn't you tell me sooner? Hurry! Are the police still here?"

"No, wait!" Nellie looked up at her with panic in her eyes. "Please don't tell the police! The Scarpellis will get in trouble!"

Hugo picked up the fallen chair, set it on its feet, and pressed Heather back down into it. "We don't think the Scarpellis have anything to do with Mandy or with Justin," he explained with a wry smile. Nellie's eyes turned back to the floor, but there was a hint of a smile playing about the corners of her mouth too. Heather's eyes darted from one to the other. What was going on between these two?

"Mrs. Scarpelli wanted to know if she could still bring Mona back to the day care center," Nellie said, "if you haven't filled Mona's place already. She said they got scared because a man knocked on their door the other night, a very strange-looking man." Nellie's eyes darted sideways at Hugo, and the little smile danced around her mouth again. "She said the man was asking all kinds of questions about the family—especially about their nephew, Luigi."

Nellie looked up at Heather. "Luigi is here illegally," she said simply. "His visa has expired, but he doesn't want to go back to Italy because he is in love with an American girl. So when this strange man came and asked questions, they got scared and moved in with Mrs. Scarpelli's brother." Nellie shrugged. "But life goes on, and they all need to work, so they must have day care for Mona."

Heather stared at Nellie, trying to see through those huge, dark eyes to what was going on in Nellie's head. "So why did they talk to *you*?" she asked suspiciously.

"I think they thought I might understand," Nellie said. "Because of my name, maybe she thought I would have family here without the right papers." She raised her chin, and her eyes flashed. "Me, I am a citizen!" she announced.

"Yes, yes, of course," Heather murmured. She looked over at Hugo, who was beaming like some kind of proud father under that pile of wild hair. He had obviously told Nellie everything about checking on the Scarpellis and the other missing families. He couldn't be trusted with a secret for more than thirty seconds!

"That red truck you saw yesterday, that wasn't the Scarpellis, was it?" Heather asked.

"A red truck?" Hugo broke in before Nellie could answer. "You said something before about a red pickup truck!"

"Yes, Hugo," Heather said impatiently. "Nellie *says* that

she saw Mandy go by on the street out front in a red truck, and Justin—"

"Was it a Dodge Ram," Hugo was asking Nellie, "a fairly new one?"

Nellie raised her shoulders helplessly. "I don't know about trucks. Yes, I think it was kind of new, but—"

"I saw that truck!" Hugo exclaimed. "Last night when I was following Nellie—" He glanced over at her, and a blush spread up from his collar and across his face until the tips of his ears were bright red. Nellie was blushing too, Heather observed. "I was standing on the corner near her apartment building, waiting while she stopped to talk to someone," Hugo rushed on. "A red Dodge Ram pulled up at the traffic light, and I was looking at it, just for something to do. I noticed that there was a word drawn in the dust on the right front fender." He paused for a moment and then added in a dramatic whisper, "It said *Hoffman*."

Heather leapt to her feet again. "Why didn't you say so before?" she shrieked.

Hugo stepped back, lifting up his hands. "Um, Heather, now that I think of it, it didn't really look like a grown-up wrote it. More like a kid, you know, maybe playing a game. Maybe it didn't actually say *Hoffman*, maybe I just—"

"Mandy!" Heather gasped. "Mandy knows her letters!"

Hugo looked over at Nellie for help, wishing he had never got this started. "But she's just a little kid, isn't she? I mean, would she know how to write someone's name?"

"I don't know! But it was a message from Justin, it has to be! I've got to call the police! Let me alone!" Heather pushed Hugo aside and hurried out of the kitchen, but Hugo followed her into her office with Nellie trailing behind.

Heather dialed 911 and demanded to be connected with the officers who had visited the day care center.

She was almost dancing with impatience as the phone clicked through.

"Mrs. Cobb?" the policewoman's voice crackled suddenly. "This is Officer Sims. I visited you with Officer Prentiss. I was just about to call you."

"Yes, yes, what did you find out?" Heather begged.

"Well, we visited the address you gave us for the Scarpellis, and they had moved out. The building superintendent said he had no idea where they had gone."

"Yes, we knew that!" Heather cried.

"And then we went to see the Hoffmans," the officer said. "Same thing."

"What do you mean?"

"They've moved out. The apartment was empty. They're gone without a trace."

Heather plopped the phone back into its cradle without saying good-bye and walked out into the main room in a daze. She walked among the children who were playing with the blocks in the middle of the room as if they weren't there. She couldn't feel her feet touching the tile floor.

A mother hurried in with a four-year-old in tow. She spoke briefly with Tina, pushed the child in the direction of the blocks, and hurried out again. Heather watched the front door swing shut behind her. It had hardly touched the door frame when it opened again for another mother and child.

Heather shook her head. People were still dropping off their children. For them, it was still early, a morning like other mornings.

She drifted back toward her office. She didn't feel like talking to anyone. But when she pushed open the door to the stuffy little room, she stopped dead.

Nellie was standing next to her desk, going through Heather's papers. Hugo stood watching her.

"Nellie!" Heather said sharply. "What do you think you're doing?"

Nellie whirled around. "I'm—I just thought—"

Heather stalked toward her. "Get away from that desk, both of you! You have no right to touch anything on my desk! This is it, Nellie! I'm going to have to let you go! And Hugo, I want you to leave right now! Whose side are you on, anyway?"

"Oh, please, Mrs. Cobb!" Nellie said. "I know I should have let you do this, but you were so troubled, and Hugo said— You see, when I wrote down the Scarpellis' new address, I remembered how there's a card for every family, with a telephone number and address for someone to call in an emergency. A family member, or a neighbor—"

"We were looking for the Hoffmans' card," Hugo chimed in. "We wanted to look at the emergency address. Maybe that's where they went! We thought it was worth a try—"

Hugo's voice trailed off when Heather didn't answer. She just stood and glared at them.

"Please, Mrs. Cobb," Nellie said, "we didn't—"

"Get out! Both of you!" was all Heather said.

Nellie melted away through the door. Hugo opened his mouth, closed it again, and shuffled out after Nellie.

Heather sat down at the desk and looked at the papers that were laid out across the top. Most of them had to do with the day care center's accounts: food, rent, payments for electricity and water, the new furnace. She couldn't imagine why Nellie would want to look at them.

The file box with all the families' cards was on the

corner of the desk. Had Nellie really been looking in it? Or had she just spotted it and made up that story as she went along? For someone who had always been so quiet, Nellie sure could talk when she got caught!

Heather's fingers tapped on the top of the file box. Then she opened the box, flipped through the cards, and pulled out the one for the Hoffmans.

The emergency number was for a Florence Hoffman at 8685 West 84th Street. She was listed as Kyle and Rory's grandmother.

Heather picked up the telephone, held it for a moment, then set it back into the cradle.

If Mandy was at Florence Hoffman's house, it would be better not to call and warn them. It would be better just to go there.

She didn't want to go by herself. But she couldn't take Hugo, not if he had gone over to Nellie's side. She just couldn't trust Hugo anymore.

Who could she call? She chewed on the side of her finger, thinking, thinking.

And then her hand reached out for the telephone again. Quickly she dialed the number for the Tates.

CHAPTER 12

Justin's feet felt like lead as he pounded across the parking lot. The only way he knew his feet were there was the shock waves they sent up to his knees. The chain-link fence looked impossibly far away. Could he make it to the hole in the fence before his feet gave out from under him?

Behind him he heard a shout, then the truck's engine revved. Out of the corner of his eye, he saw the truck swerve toward him. It was going to cut him off!

He stretched out his long legs and ran with everything he had in him. His feet burst into flames of pain as the blood began to flow into them again, but he pushed the pain out of his mind and thought about nothing except the gap in the fence. He willed the gap to come closer, closer.

The truck behind him was closer too. The sound of its engine beat against his ears.

It was gaining on him.

Would they stop and jump out to grab him? Or would they just keep coming at full speed and squash him against the fence like a bug?

He ran. Oh, he ran. The fence was close enough now that he could see the chain links gleaming in the early-morning sunlight. Each square of the fence seemed to stare back at him like a little eye. The broken links looked sharp and clear where they bent back on themselves. Only a few more steps—

The truck roared behind him like a tornado, swallowing him up in its noise. It wasn't going to stop!

Justin's heart felt as if it would burst in his chest. Two more steps, one more—He flung himself forward toward the hole, slammed onto the pavement on the other side of the fence, and rolled aside.

Behind him, the air was shattered by the squeal of brakes. Gravel spattered over him as the truck skittered sideways, then swerved in a tight curve back toward the parking lot entrance.

As Justin dragged himself to his knees, the breath rattled in and out of his chest in great gasps. At the ends of his legs, his feet burned as if he had stuck them into boiling water. Where the rope had cut into his ankles there were bands of pain like slices of a knife. He was totally exhausted.

He staggered onto his feet. The truck was already nearing the parking lot entrance. When they got to the street, it wouldn't take them a moment to turn and come at him. He glanced back through the gap in the fence. If he dove through again, it would only buy him a few seconds. There was no place to go inside the parking lot.

In the next instant he was dashing across the street.

In front of him was an abandoned warehouse—or what was left of it. The whole end wall was gone, leaving the huge building yawning open like the dark mouth of a cave. He dove in.

Empty crates and huge splinters of wood from the warehouse wall clutched at his legs as he worked his way into the clear space in the middle of the building. It was darker with every step farther from the open wall but he pushed onward away from the street.

Behind him the street echoed with the sound of an engine grinding by in low gear. Tires squealed as the Dodge turned around in sharp jabs, and back it came. It stopped outside the open wall of the warehouse. Justin dropped down behind a broken crate and crouched there, waiting for whatever would happen next.

Nothing happened next. Out on the street there was only the sound of the truck's engine idling.

Justin listened, his ears pricked up like an animal's to gather in any sound of footsteps, of someone coming. He fought down the impulse to stick his head up above the edge of the crate to see what was going on. If he made any motion, he knew they'd spot him.

Now there was a shout in the distance—Mack's voice, Justin guessed. The truck shifted into gear and pulled away. It wouldn't be more than a minute or two before whoever was in the truck got Mack untied from his car and came back. And now there would be Mack to help with the search. And Mack was going to be angry. He would not be satisfied until he had finished what he had started.

He would not be satisfied until Justin was dead.

Justin looked around him, trying to figure out what to do next. There was no way he could go back out the way he had come in. The open wall of the warehouse faced the spot where Mack's Bonneville sat in the parking lot. They'd be watching for him while they untied Mack.

Justin pushed his way onward through the debris on

the warehouse floor. The dark shapes around him were mostly empty wooden crates, old and dry and splintery. When he pushed at them, they gave way easily and scraped noisily across the uneven wooden floor.

He had to find a place to hide! But there was no place except these empty crates, and he doubted that Mack would rest until he had looked inside every single crate in the warehouse.

He worked his way farther and farther from the bright space that was the front of the warehouse. There must be a back door somewhere—

There! Twenty feet in front of him, strips of light in the darkness outlined a rectangular shape: the cracks around a door. A rush of hope flooded over him. He scuttled toward it, clambering over broken slats and boxes in his rush to be out of there.

Suddenly there was the sound of an engine outside and a squeak of brakes and tires on pavement as a vehicle stopped short. In the next instant, a car door slammed.

Justin froze, staring hypnotized at the rectangle of light, expecting at any moment to see the door jerked open from the outside. Where would he go?

Footsteps sounded outside on the pavement, then stopped. Justin looked wildly around him for a hiding space. He moved, crouching cat-like, toward a large crate that lay on its side behind several smaller ones to the right of the door. He crawled into the crate and huddled, heart pounding, straining to listen. Waiting.

Away in the front of the warehouse the truck door slammed. They had the front and back of the building guarded. Justin was pinned.

He crouched on all fours inside the crate like an animal. Dust swirled up around him, tickling his nose, settling like ashes inside his throat.

Then a familiar smell trickled into the dusty air of the crate. Cigarette smoke. Like in the garage.

That meant that Mack was right outside the door, standing at his ease, smoking.

Suddenly anger shot through Justin. First they'd had him tied in that garage, and then in the trunk of Mack's car, and now they had him cooped up in an empty packing crate while Mack stood around having a cigarette! *If I ever got out of this alive, I'll—*

With a creaking groan the back door was wrenched open, and heavy footsteps thudded on the wooden floorboards.

Crash! Something slammed against the crate Justin was hiding in. He caught his breath at the jolt and ground his teeth together to keep himself from crying out. Crash! Crash! Mack was picking up the empty crates and throwing them. If he tried to heave the one where Justin was crouching, he'd know in an instant it wasn't empty!

"Did you find anything?" called a voice from the front of the warehouse.

"No, nothing!" snarled Mack's voice. "There's nothing back here but a bunch of old crates."

"They're all over the place! The whole warehouse is full of them!" called the other voice. It was Hoffman. Justin hoped there weren't any others, that the rest of Hoffman's buddies had meant what they said and stayed out of the picture. He might still have a chance against two of them.

"He's in here somewhere!" came Mack's voice again— almost directly over Justin's head. Justin's heart clenched. He could almost feel Mack's huge, meaty paws reaching for the edge of the crate above him, or his enormous boot hauling back to deliver a kick to the thin wooden slats that were all that separated the two of them.

"Well, without a flashlight this could take all day!"

shouted Hoffman. "It's only a matter of time before some cop comes snooping by. Come on! I'm getting out of here!"

"Wait a minute, boss! I've got an idea!" Justin could hear Mack moving around near him. A crate scraped across the floor. Suddenly there was the sound of wood splintering.

"What are you doing?" called Hoffman.

"Go back outside. I'll get him to come out, you'll see."

Fear knifed Justin's guts. He didn't know what Mack was up to, so near him in the dark, but he knew he wasn't going to like it. Because Mack's voice sounded—

Satisfied.

And then there was the *snick* of a match.

In the darkness, Justin saw the glow of the first tiny flame. The glow increased quickly, grew higher, bigger, like something alive. The flames crackled in the dry wood as if they were laughing at some evil joke.

The fire leapt from crate to crate, gaining strength as it found new fuel. As the flames danced higher and higher, the crates and their shadows jumped and flickered all around him. Already Justin could feel the heat. He had to move—now.

He crawled out of the crate he had been hiding in and stuck his head up over the edge. He could see Mack's hulking form poking up out of the smoke, lit by the orange glow of the flames. His body filled the back doorway of the warehouse. In his hand was a gun.

Justin looked toward the open front of the warehouse. He didn't know if Hoffman was still guarding that way out. But it didn't matter—there was no way he could get out the front. The fire was already ahead of him.

The heat was pushing him to move. He moved the only way he could move, along the back wall of the warehouse, toward the corner, crouching low, dodging from crate to crate. He didn't know where he was going or what he would do when he got to the corner. He only knew that he had to get away from the heat and smoke.

Suddenly he realized that he was dropping lower. He was below the level of the smoke—below the level of the warehouse floor. He couldn't understand—but he kept moving.

He was no longer dropping now, but he was so far down that he could stand upright with his head almost below the level of the floor. Beside him was a wall, the side wall of this slot he had walked down into. He moved onward along the slot, step by step, through broken crates and big pieces of metal and other debris. Beside him brackets on the wall still held a few tools.

With a quick leap of hope, he realized where he was. In the days when this warehouse was still used, this passageway would lead under the loading dock where the trucks pulled in. Mechanics would use this passageway to work under the trucks.

Outside. The truck would be outside. On the side street, out of sight of the back door of the warehouse.

Yes—now he was bending down to pass under the outside wall of the warehouse. Above him was air and light and the beautiful blue sky.

He gripped the upper edge of the passageway and pulled himself up onto the pavement in front of the loading dock. At his back the fire roared inside the warehouse and smoke billowed out into the air above his head. In front of him was nothing but the empty street and more warehouses in the distance. He had to get out of sight. But where? How?

Beside him was a tiny toolshed. He dodged around it to find the door. Hot in there, too hot to stay. Maybe there would be an old wrench or something that he could use as a weapon.

Better than a weapon—leaning against the wall of the toolshed, abandoned and dusty but just waiting for someone to need it, was a bicycle. Quicker than thought, he was on the bicycle and out on the street.

The handlebars were warm under his hands. The pedals creaked and wobbled as they turned. But he was moving.

He cut to the right—he'd rather take his chances with Hoffman than with Mack—and pedaled as fast as he could. He shot around the corner and cut left down the street, away from the burning warehouse. He raced for the next intersection, aiming to turn up the side street and put another warehouse between him and Hoffman. As he pedaled, his ears strained for the angry shout behind him. His back waited for the *thunk* of a bullet.

None came. He reached the intersection and whipped around the corner, glancing back at the warehouse Mack had set ablaze.

Flames leaped high above the roof. What was left of the front wall suddenly fell forward into the street in a red-hot display of sparks and burning splinters. Smoke rolled up into the sky in a tall black column.

Far off, a siren began to blow. The fire had been spotted. Soon the whole area would be full of fire trucks and police cars and news reporters asking questions.

Justin sped down the side street, away from the fire. By some instinct, he knew he had to move fast. Not because of what he had seen in front of the warehouse, but because of what he had not seen.

The red Dodge pickup truck had disappeared.

CHAPTER
13

Justin pedaled down the street as fast as he could push the poor old bicycle. As he crossed the next intersection, he looked along the side street toward the burning warehouse. He saw Mack's old Bonneville still parked by the back door, and beyond it Mack was standing in the street staring toward the approaching sirens. But there was no sign of Hoffman or the Dodge Ram.

He kept pedaling. He figured he was running parallel to the main street, the street that the fire trucks would come in on. Hoffman must be on the main street too, speeding off in the other direction. He wouldn't want to be standing around watching the warehouse burn when the fire trucks arrived. Justin hoped that just maybe Mack was too stupid—or too stubborn—to make a getaway.

The old bicycle creaked and groaned underneath him. The back tire was rubbing against the rear fender. He ought to get off and bend the fender out to get it off the tire, but he couldn't spare a moment. Let it grind!

He whipped across another intersection and looked left across the side street. The main street was still empty. No sign of the Dodge Ram.

Ahead of him, the ranks of warehouses began to give way to factories. There were cars on the street and people out on the sidewalks. Most of them were gawking at the fire, pointing, shouting to each other, beginning to hustle over to get a better look. Justin hoped they wouldn't notice one guy on a bicycle beating it in the other direction.

The street ahead of him became an obstacle course. Cars and trucks stopped short as the drivers spotted the fire. People drifted off the sidewalks into the street with their eyes on the flames leaping into the sky a few blocks away. Justin dodged around them, trying to keep watch for Hoffman's truck.

Then suddenly there it was, crossing the next intersection right in front of him! Justin jerked the bicycle to the right to hide behind a tractor-trailer truck.

Had Hoffman seen him? Justin didn't have time to worry about it. He yanked upward on the handlebars, popped the bicycle up onto the sidewalk, and cut around the corner after the Dodge.

Where was Hoffman going? He didn't seem to be heading back toward his apartment and the garages down on Edgemont Street. Right now he was pointed at the west side. Was he just putting some distance between himself and the fire trucks—or did he have someplace in mind?

The sirens screamed closer and closer. The street was packed now with people and cars. Justin cut in and out, weaving through the traffic, fighting to keep the truck in view, watching for that flash of red.

But they were leaving the excitement behind them. If Hoffman got a clear road, Justin knew that he wouldn't be able to keep up with the truck on this old bicycle.

He had to. Somehow he knew that he just had to.

*   *   *

Henry Tate parked his battered Ford in front of the little house on West 84th Street, but he kept his hand on the key in the ignition. "Do you really think this is a good idea?" he asked.

Heather gazed at the neat little house set square in its tidy little yard. It was painted white with green shutters, and it had flowers already blooming out front and a carefully swept brick walk leading to the front door. Everything about it said *Welcome*. It was just the kind of house that she and Justin dreamed of having after the baby was born. "I think it'll be all right," she said. "You'll be right here. If anything goes wrong, it won't take you a moment to get in there."

"I really think I should come in with you—"

"No, it's better if you stay out here to keep watch, just in case. She might not open the door to a strange man, even in broad daylight, but if she sees a pregnant woman on her doorstep, she won't worry for a moment. She'll let me in." Heather turned toward Henry, her eyes large and serious. "We've got to know if Mandy is in that house."

Henry Tate nodded. Then as Heather reached for the door handle, he gripped her arm. "Just be careful," he said.

Heather looked once more toward the house, then opened the car door. She heaved herself out of the car, pushed the door shut, and lumbered up the front walk.

She shivered as she stood on the welcome mat. *It's still early*, she told herself, *still a little chilly out*. She knocked on the freshly painted door, just below the three little windows that marched in a diagonal line down the upper half of the panel.

A pair of eyes appeared in the lowest window, topped by a heap of white curls. The eyes looked at her carefully.

Heather was suddenly aware of more eyes watching her. A pile of little faces was pressed against the bottom of a window near the door, just beyond the green shutter. Heather recognized Kyle and Rory. And the other face, behind them, just barely visible through the glare of the window glass—was that Mandy? Heather's breath caught inside her ribs. *Oh, please, let that be Mandy!*

The door opened slowly. "May I help you?" asked a gentle voice.

The woman standing quietly, one hand on the doorknob, was smaller than Heather, somewhat stooped but slim. She was in her late sixties, Heather judged, with blue-white hair so tightly curled that she looked as if she had just come from a session at the beauty parlor. She wore dark green slacks and a dark green sweater, and she looked exhausted.

"Mrs. Hoffman?" Heather asked. "I'm Heather Cobb, and I'm the director of the Little Friends Day Care Center where Kyle and Rory have been enrolled. They've suddenly stopped coming, and since no one had called, we were a bit concerned, and—"

"Mrs. Cobb!" screeched a young voice from inside the house. A tiny bundle of energy shot out of the house and threw itself against her, almost pushing her backwards off the doorstep.

Heather regained her balance and peered around her stomach at the little person who was now hugging her tightly around the knees. "Well, hello, Rory!" she laughed. "I'm glad to see you too!"

Another little boy danced in the doorway. "Mrs. Cobb! Mrs. Cobb!" he sang. "Take us back to the day care! I want to play with the blocks!"

"Well, Kyle, those blocks are lonely without you!" Heather assured him. Hoping she seemed to be just looking at him, she tried to peer around Mrs. Hoffman to see if she could spot Mandy. "I hope you can come back to Little Friends soon!"

"To tell you the truth, Mrs. Cobb, I wish you could take the three of them back with you right now! They're just too much for me to handle!" Mrs. Hoffman sighed.

This was the lead Heather needed. "Three of them?" she asked.

Mrs. Hoffman's eyes widened. "Oh, dear! I wasn't supposed to tell anyone—I mean—"

"Oh, that's fine, Mrs. Hoffman," Heather said smoothly. "You have Mandy Tate visiting with you, isn't that right? I'm sure it's perfectly fine that you have all three of them."

Mrs. Hoffman looked relieved. "Well, if you already knew that Mandy was here, then that must be all right. Would you like to come in and sit down? I shouldn't leave you standing on the doorstep in your condition!" Glancing toward the car parked at the curb, she added, "Would Mr. Cobb like to come in too?"

Heather smiled. "I think the gentleman in the car would love to come in," she said.

The next few minutes were a whirlwind of tears and hugs and laughter and more hugs. When she saw her father, Mandy let out a whoop of pure joy and threw herself into his arms. "Papa, you came back!" she cried, completely forgetting that she was the one who had taken off.

"Yes, darling, oh my beautiful darling, I'm here!" He held her close up under his chin in his great arms and rocked her as if she had been a tiny baby. "Oh, my sweet precious girl!"

"Oh, she's found her papa!" Mrs. Hoffman said excitedly. "I didn't know the poor little thing was lost! She's been so brave, never cried, not even once! Oh, this is wonderful!" Her grandsons danced around them, shouting with happiness, as if they had been the ones lost

and now found. Heather laughed out loud to see them all
so happy. She looked about the toy-littered living room,
half expecting to see Justin pop out of one of the other
rooms to find out what the fuss was all about.

"Where's Mama?" Mandy asked, her shrill voice rising
above all the others. "I want my mama!"

"She's at home by the telephone, sweetheart, just
waiting in case anyone calls. And I think that should be
us! Ma'am," he said, turning to Mrs. Hoffman, "could we
use your telephone? I just want to call my wife."

"Oh, yes, she'll want to hear from you!" Mrs. Hoffman
said gaily. "It's right through there in the kitchen, on the
wall next to the—"

"What on earth is going on here?" demanded a gruff
voice.

Silence fell over the roomful of people like a great
weight. They all turned to look at the man standing in
the open doorway, feet planted, his face purple with rage.

"Daddy!" cried Kyle. He liked the excitement of being
found. He wanted to be a found person too.

"Daddy, we're here!" Rory chimed in. Whatever his
older brother did, he had to follow.

"Ken, look, we've found this little girl's father!" Mrs.
Hoffman exclaimed.

"Shut up!" Hoffman shouted at them all. "Mom, I told
you not to let anyone in! Not *anyone*!"

Mrs. Hoffman's face was a mixture of confusion and
annoyance. "I know you did, but these people— Oh, Ken,
you really shouldn't talk that way!"

"Mr. Hoffman, we've just come to pick up Mandy,"
Heather said. "That's all we want." She tried to make her
voice sound firm, but inside her whole body felt like
water. How could she have been so *stupid?* They should

have got out of there the minute they got hold of
Mandy! This man was a kidnapper! Was he alone, or were
there others all around the house? There had been time
for a whole gang of them to get into position while she
and Henry Tate jumped around like idiots inside the
house with no one watching the street. "All we want is
Mandy," she repeated, "so now we will leave, and there
will be no questions asked."

The little boys stared up at their father open-mouthed
like a pair of baby birds in a nest. Mrs. Hoffman looked
at her son with narrowed eyes, as if she was wondering
who he really was. Henry Tate clutched his daughter to
him and waited, his face like stone. The little living room
filled with silence like a tub filling up with water.

"There will be no questions asked," Heather said again.
Oh, but there was one question she wanted to ask: *Where
is Justin?* But she did not dare even speak his name. She
stood in silence, waiting, holding back the tears that
welled up in her eyes.

A long minute went by. Then, without a word, Hoffman
stepped away from the doorway to let them pass.

Heather glanced toward Mrs. Hoffman, and then at
each of the little boys, saying a silent farewell. Then she
and Henry Tate walked toward the open doorway, toward
the bright sunshine of the spring morning.

Suddenly the doorway went dark. The space was filled
with the huge body of a young man who stood with his
muscular arms crossed, glaring in at them. In one of his great
paws, lying ready against the other forearm, he held a gun.

"Nobody's going anywhere," said Mack.

CHAPTER 14

Justin had to admit it: he'd lost Hoffman. And he was too tired to push this rusty old bicycle another minute. He pulled over to the curb and leaned against a parked car, panting.

He was too tired to think. In fact, his whole body wanted to drop to the pavement and just lie there and rest, parked against the curb for the day like just a car.

When he rubbed his hands over his face, they came away black with soot. He looked down at his clothes, filthy from the night in the trunk of Mack's Bonneville and crusted with dirt and soot from the fire in the warehouse. People must think he was an old bum who'd spent the night under a newspaper in the park.

What he wanted to do was go home and clean up and sleep, forget all about Hoffman and Mack and Mandy Tate. But Hoffman and Mack weren't going to forget.

He had to figure things out. And Heather. Heather

would be worried sick. At least he owed her a phone call. He dragged the bicycle up onto the sidewalk and pushed it toward a pay phone on the corner.

"Oh, hello, Mr. Cobb," said Tina's cheerful voice at the day care center. "No, Mrs. Cobb's not here. She talked with the police for awhile, and then she went somewhere with Mr. Tate. I don't know what it was all about, but she seemed pretty excited."

Justin's stomach clenched. "What about Nellie? Does she know where Heather is?"

"Um, Nellie's not here any more."

"What do you mean? Did she go with Heather?"

"No, I mean she doesn't work here any more. You see, Mrs. Cobb fired Nellie this morning, and Nellie went off with some guy with really weird hair."

Hugo! How did Hugo fit into all this? "Tina, what did—"

"Jason, stop that!" Tina shouted suddenly. "You've got to share! Those blocks are for everybody!"

"When Heather gets back, just tell her I called, okay?" Justin said.

"Okay, Mr. Cobb. Bye!"

He rested for another moment against the side of the phone booth. It looked as if Heather had figured out where Mandy was. He was glad that Tina said she'd got the police in on it, but he wished she'd left it up to them. He didn't like the idea of her being on the scene at the Hoffmans' place at all, even with Mandy's father there to look after her.

Well, for right now there was nothing he could do about any of it. He just wanted to go home and get cleaned up, maybe lie on his bed and stare at the ceiling for awhile. Without a backward glance at the rusty old bicycle, he walked two blocks over to Randall Street, dug some change from his pocket, and got on the next bus that came along.

The bus driver stared straight ahead through the windshield as Justin stepped up onto the bus, but the other passengers gave him don't-you-dare-sit-next-to-*me* looks as he walked down the aisle and threw himself into a seat. *Okay!* he wanted to shout at them. *I know I'm a mess, but if you'd been through a night like I've had . . .*

The bus crawled along toward midtown. A few more blocks and he'd be passing near the day care center and almost home. He'd call Heather again as soon as he got in. He did hope they'd found Mandy, he really did. But it didn't seem fair, after all he'd gone through, that they'd found her without him, and it was all over.

He leaned his forehead against the bus window, almost asleep. As his eyes drifted shut, they fell on two figures on the sidewalk: a slim young woman who walked so quietly that the long rope of dark hair down her back hardly moved, and slouching along beside her, a guy in clothes worse than Justin's. Hugo! And that must be Nellie!

Justin yanked the stop cord on the bus and dove down the aisle. As he leapt off the bus at the next corner, Hugo was telling Nellie something, talking so fast that his whole body jerked with the effort. He flung out his arms in a wide gesture and jabbed an elderly man coming the other way.

The old man staggered backwards, stabbing about with his cane to regain his balance. "Here's another one!" the old man snapped as Justin dashed up beside them. "Just look at the way you young people dress these days! No pride at all!" He stamped off, whacking the sidewalk with his cane.

"Nellie! Where's Heather?" Justin asked. "What's going on?"

"Heather fired her!" Hugo announced before Nellie could answer. "Nellie was the one who figured out where Mandy was, but Heather up and fired her, just like that!"

Justin slashed the air with his hand. *"Where is Heather?"*

"We thought Mandy might be with the Hoffman

children—at their grandmother's house," Nellie faltered.

"Yes! Grandma Hoffman's house! That's where Mandy said she and the other kids stayed during the day!" Justin exclaimed. "So the police are on their way, right?"

"No, I think just Mrs. Cobb and Mr. Tate—"

"You sent her to face the Hoffmans *alone*?" Justin shouted. "First you set me up! You sent me off after that pickup truck so Hoffman and Mack could jump me—and now Heather! You're right in it with them, aren't you?"

Nellie cringed back against Hugo. "I—"

"Nellie's doing the best she can," Hugo snapped, putting his arm around Nellie's shoulders, "and look what thanks she gets!"

Justin stared at him. "Now she's got you too, Hugo? No!" With a cry of rage, he ran off down the street.

Hugo and Nellie ran after him. "Justin! Wait!"

Justin spotted a policeman on the opposite corner of the intersection and dove into the traffic as if it were water. A car lurched to a stop in a squeal of brakes just inches from him, he ran straight on, almost slamming into the side of a car passing the other way. Another car swerved out around him, and horn blasts and angry shouts filled the air.

Hugo grabbed Nellie's hand and dragged her into the street with him. For an instant, the gap that Justin had forced in the traffic stayed open, and they dashed through it behind him.

All three arrived on the opposite corner in a heap almost on top of the policeman. "Are you crazy, all three of you?" he bellowed. "If you were *trying* to cause an accident, you sure picked a good way to do it!"

"My wife!" Justin panted. "My wife's in trouble! She's gone to this old lady's house, only her son—the old lady's son—has been dealing in stolen goods, and he's got a gun—well, this other guy's got a gun, and they—"

"Whoa, slow down!" the policeman said. He looked at Justin's dirt-streaked bicycle jacket and wrinkled slacks, then swung his eyes over Hugo's tattered lumberjack shirt, down to his high-top sneakers with bits of knotted string for laces, and back up to his Albert Einstein hairdo. "Yeah, I guess anyone's who's married to either one of you *is* in trouble."

"They've gone to—to—What's the address?" Justin begged Nellie.

Nellie crunched her eyes shut, trying to remember. "I think it was 86-something West 84th Street, a long way out."

"Hoffman!" Justin said. "The guy's name is Ken Hoffman, and he's got some guy working for him named Mack!"

"Yeah, yeah, that's fine," the policeman said. "Look, whatever you guys are on, it's not good for your mental processes." He yawned. "You're lucky it's time for my coffee break, or I'd run all three of you in for jaywalking. Take it a little easy crossing the street, okay?" Tucking his radio further into his belt, he ambled away toward a coffee shop two doors down on the side street.

"He's not even going to report it!" Justin howled. "I've got to go to her!" Frantically, he scanned the passing traffic. "There's never a taxi when you really need one!"

"Your car's back at the day care center!" Hugo offered. "I saw it in the alley out back."

"My car!" Justin scrabbled in his pocket and yanked out a set of keys. "They never took my keys away!" He was already running in the direction of the day care center. Hugo and Nellie were pulled along behind him as if they were caught in the wind of his slipstream.

*   *   *

As they rushed through the traffic toward the west side, Justin told Hugo about his day in the chair in Hoffman's garage and his escape from Mack and the warehouse fire. "Holy cow!" Hugo said over and over, obviously burning with jealousy that he'd missed all the real action.

Justin glanced in the rearview mirror at Nellie, who sat on the backseat listening to his story without a word of comment. Why had Hugo insisted on bringing her along?

They found West 84th Street and counted down to the 8600 block. "That must be the house, the little white one," Hugo said in a low voice. "I think that is Tate's car, the blue one, parked across the street. And that is Hoffman's pickup truck parked out front, isn't it?" he added. "We've got trouble, don't we?"

"We've got big trouble," Justin agreed. He'd seen something else. Right behind the blue car on the other side of the street was a rusty old Bonneville.

Justin shot down to the end of the street and cut around that corner and the next one until he figured they were lined up with the back of Grandma Hoffman's house. In a moment he was trotting through the neighbor's backyard with Hugo and Nellie on his heels.

He halted, using the neighbor's garage for cover, and stared at the back of Mrs. Hoffman's house as if he could see right through the walls. "You stay here," he whispered. "I'm going to have a look!" He sprinted across the strip of grass separating the neighbor's garage from Mrs. Hoffman's and then dove for the shrubbery under the windows on the side of the house. Slowly he lifted his head to peer over the windowsill.

Hoffman stood with his back to the window. Beyond him was Tate, holding Mandy, who had her skinny little arms wrapped his neck so tightly he probably couldn't breathe. An older woman stood in the middle of the floor, wringing her hands and crying, while two little boys clung to her, one on each leg. But where was Mack? And where was Heather?

"What do you see?" whispered a voice under his elbow.

"Hugo!" Justin hissed. "I told you to stay back!"

Hugo's head lifted slowly beside Justin's like a second sunrise. "Who's the big guy?"

Justin squinted at the scene on the other side of the glass. Now he could see Mack's tree trunk of a leg and one huge arm. The big paw at the end of the arm was holding a gun.

"That's my good buddy Mack," Justin whispered. "A good man with a rope. Not too bad with matches, either. Can you see Heather?"

Just then Hoffman took a step toward his mother, and Justin could see Heather sitting on a couch at the far side of the room. Her head lolled back against the back of the couch and her arms cradled her belly as if she was trying to protect her unborn baby from all the evil that was surging around it. Justin's heart leapt out to her. *Oh, Heather—*

"What are we going to do?" whispered Hugo.

"I'll go around to the back. You knock on the door and pretend—"

"But they've seen me! Remember the census-taker scam? They'd know they've seen me before. People always do!"

"Yeah, I'll bet," Justin sighed. "Then what—"

"I'll go," murmured a tiny voice beside him.

"Nellie, no!" Hugo hissed. "It's not safe!"

Justin looked down at Nellie. Crouched down at his side under the window, she looked like a little child. But, oh, the trouble she'd caused! "I think she might be plenty safe in there—with her friends!" he snarled.

"Mr. Cobb, you've got to trust me," Nellie said.

Just then, inside the house, Tate turned slightly so that Mandy was facing the window over his shoulder. Her eyes widened. She'd spotted them. *Don't say anything!* Justin willed her. *Don't let on—*

"We've got to make our move *now*," Justin said between gritted teeth. "Nellie, I guess I do have to trust you. I have to admit, they never acted like they knew you. And you're our only chance."

Justin picked up a good-sized rock that was lying next to the foundation of the house, hefted it in his hand for weight, handed it to Hugo, and picked up a second one. "When I nod my head, break this window and go in as fast as you can. I'll go in this one over here. Throw the rock downward, so the kids don't get hit with the glass. Okay, Nellie. Knock on the front door."

Nellie crawled beyond the view of the window and straightened up, her head high, her face calm. She reached for Hugo's hand and squeezed it. Then she walked without a backwards glance, without a tremor, toward the front door and knocked.

"What was that?" Mack's voice snarled from inside the house.

Justin crouched, ready to spring. He held up his hand to Hugo. *Wait—*

Nellie knocked again.

"Someone's at the door," Mrs. Hoffman said, her voice quavering.

"So answer it!" Mack growled. "But be careful!"

"Go ahead, Mom," Hoffman said.

The door creaked open.

"Now!" Justin cried. He and Hugo threw their rocks at the same moment. As the windows burst apart in a shower of broken glass, they flung themselves through the jagged gaps and into the room.

"What the—?" Hoffman bellowed. Hugo leapt for him and knocked him backwards against the wall. His head hit first with a sickening thud, and he slid to the floor.

"Stand back! I've got him!" Mack shouted. The gun came up and swung around to point at Justin.

"No!" Heather screamed.

A chair whistled through the air and cracked against the side of Mack's head. Tate hauled off, gripping the chair by its back, and swung again, bringing it down in a powerful blow against Mack's arm. The gun flew out of Mack's hand and across the carpet. As Mack slumped, Tate pushed him down with the chair and pegged him to the floor. He still held Mandy tight in his left arm, and her arms were wrapped tightly around his neck.

"Good work!" Justin said. He turned toward the couch where Heather was slumped. "Darling, are you all right?"

"Oh, Justin," she sobbed, "I thought they'd killed you!"

Justin dropped onto the couch beside her and gathered her into his arms. "Everything's all right now," he crooned. "Everything's all right."

"Mrs. Cobb," Mandy said in a thin clear voice over Tate's shoulder, "Mrs. Cobb, Uncle Ken has a gun."

All eyes turned toward Hoffman. He stood wavering slightly as if still dizzy from being knocked against the wall. But his hands were steady. The gun he held against Hugo's ribs didn't waver at all.

CHAPTER 15

There was absolute silence in Grandma Hoffman's tidy little living room. No one moved. For a long moment, no one so much as breathed.

Except for the gun and the shards of broken glass littering the hallway, they could have been a photograph of a family gathering. The pale blue walls, the flowered curtains tied back neatly at each window, the couch with a handmade afghan draped across the back, the pair of armchairs facing a small television set, all looked so normal surrounding the children, parents, and grandmother. But they seemed to be locked together in a picture from which they could not escape.

When someone finally spoke, it was Heather. From the couch in the corner, very quietly she said, "Put the gun down, Mr. Hoffman."

Hoffman's eyes slid over to lock with hers across the crowded room. The gun stayed firmly in Hugo's back.

"Mr. Hoffman, your children are here. Your mother is here," Heather said.

From the floor, Mack let out a low moan. Tate glanced down at him, and pressed down more firmly on the chair that pinned him to the floor. Justin felt Heather's muscles go rigid within the circle of his arm, but her voice remained calm, unhurried.

"Mr. Hoffman, we can all tell that you took good care of Mandy while she was with you. You treated her as one of your own children. You never left her alone. You asked your own mother, the grandmother of your children, to care for her when you couldn't. Mandy likes you very much. She calls you Uncle Ken. Your children love you and look up to you, Mr. Hoffman."

Mack moaned again and stirred. His eyes opened, and he stared up through the rungs of the chair at Tate as if he was trying to sort out what he was seeing. His chest heaved upward against the legs of the chair. Tate had to grab the back of the chair with both hands now to keep it in place, straining until his knuckles turned white against Mack's heaves and kicks. Mandy wrapped her legs around her father's waist and clung to him like a sea creature attached to a rock.

Hoffman's eyes never left Heather's, although by his expression everyone knew that he was listening to Mack's struggle with Tate.

"Mr. Hoffman," Heather said again, "put down the gun."

"No!" Mack bellowed suddenly. "Don't do it, boss!" His huge arm lifted like a crane and flung the chair aside. Tate yanked the chair back and lunged forward with it, but Mack rolled away out from under it, grabbed the chair by one leg, and twisted it out of Tate's grip. Tate's hands grappled with thin air as he reached and reached again for the chair, but he couldn't see well enough with

Mandy tucked under his chin, and the chair was Mack's.

Mack pulled himself up and stood with his feet planted on the rug, grinning. "Good going, boss," he said.

Hoffman didn't look at him. His mouth worked noiselessly, as if he was trying to talk but couldn't make the words come. Then he said, "Mom, boys, I'm very sorry that you had to see this. I hope that in time you will be able to forget this and forgive me."

He turned his head and looked at his mother and then down at his two sons. "I am not a gunman," he said. "I should never have listened to Mack in the first place. Right now is a good time to stop."

His eyes drooped shut. His head bent forward until his chin rested against his chest. Bit by bit the gun dropped away from Hugo's back until it was pointed at the floor.

With a roar, Mack lunged toward him.

At the same moment, a huge voice cracked like thunder: "Police! The house is surrounded! No one move!"

Startled, Mack whirled toward the window. Hugo jumped for him as if he had been spring-loaded and slammed head-first into his massive shoulder. Mack staggered, off-balance, then lunged again toward Hoffman.

This time, Hoffman was ready for him. The gun came up as if it were flying under its own power and the barrel smashed across Mack's face. Mack went down like a tree across the soft blue carpet. Justin leapt to sit astride his stomach, but there was no need. Mack lay glowering up at Hoffman with eyes smoldering with hate and did not move.

"Police!" thundered the voice again from outside. "The house is surrounded. Throw out your weapons!"

Hoffman lifted his head as if waking from a deep sleep, turned, and walked slowly toward the broken window. He raised his hands slowly and gently tossed the gun out the window into the yard. "There are no other weapons," he called out. "And please be advised that there are women and children in this house."

Police burst into the house from all directions. The house churned with bodies in blue uniforms. Voices shouted orders, demanded answers, asked if Heather and Mrs. Hoffman and the children were all right. Hands reached out for Hoffman's arms, and handcuffs snapped around his wrists.

"Kenneth Hoffman, you are hereby under arrest for the kidnapping of Mandy Tate. We have also searched your garages in the alley off Edgemont Street and found goods in your possession which have been reported stolen. You have the right to remain silent. You have the right to a lawyer. Anything you say may be used against you."

Meanwhile other officers shoved to and fro in the small room, pulling Mack to his feet and reading him his rights, questioning Henry Tate, sorting out Heather and Justin and Mrs. Hoffman. Handcuffs clinked amid the windstorm of voices. Two officers started to lead Hoffman away.

"Hey!" shouted Hugo.

"Hey!" shouted Justin. "Wait a minute! Wait a minute!"

The noise subsided. The officers with Hoffman paused to look at Justin.

"Ken Hoffman didn't kidnap Mandy!" Justin said loudly. "Mandy slipped away from the day care center on her own because she wanted to go home with the Hoffman kids. The Hoffmans took good care of her and tried to find a way to get her back to the day care center. But this guy—" Justin jerked a thumb in Mack's direction. "You'll want to book him for attempted murder and for arson in the warehouse fire on the north side this morning. I am an eyewitness."

"What about her?" an officer asked, pointing at Nellie. "How does she fit in?"

Justin hesitated. "She's an employee of the day care center," he said carefully. "She has been very concerned about Mandy's disappearance."

"Tell them about me!" Hugo squawked from behind him.

Justin turned to see Hugo in handcuffs, flanked by two large officers. "Believe it or not," Justin said, suddenly choking with relieved laughter, "he's with me."

"Mrs. Hoffman," Tate said in a low voice, "I'm sorry for all the trouble my Mandy has caused. But could I use your telephone to call my wife?"

Mrs. Hoffman, watching her son being led away, nodded absentmindedly. Heather leaned her head against Justin's shoulder. "I feel so bad for them," she murmured.

Justin rubbed his hands over the welts that the ropes had left on his wrists. He would probably never tell Heather all of it. "Hoffman was right," he said simply. "He should never have listened to Mack."

*   *   *

"You should let me take you home," Justin told Heather for the fourth or fifth time as they drove back toward the day care center. "You're exhausted! You need to rest!"

"I've got to get back!" Heather told him again. "Nellie and I left Tina alone with all those children. There should be at least two people on duty at all times! Besides," she added, stroking the back of his hand where it lay on the steering wheel, "I feel fine now that we've got Mandy back. And you."

When Justin parked in the alley in back of the day care building, he fussed about for a moment trying to brush some of the dirt off his clothes, and Hugo and Nellie seemed to be very busy gazing into each others' eyes in the back seat. So it was Heather who pushed open the back door of the building and stepped quietly into the kitchen.

What she saw was Tina's large backside bent over in front of the open refrigerator. The huge red roses on Tina's skirt looked as if they were swaying on their stalks as Tina leaned deep into the refrigerator to reach for something in the very back. Heather had watched Justin in the same act so many times—he always thought the best stuff must be in the very back of the refrigerator—but his skinny rump had never looked like a field of flowers. Heather giggled at the thought.

Tina whirled around and gaped at Heather, a five-pound block of cheese clutched in her hand. She slowly straightened up, holding the cheese in front of her like a shield. "I was just—You weren't back yet, so I thought I'd better see what there was for the children's lunch, and—"

Heather's eyes narrowed as the final piece of the mystery clicked into place. "You know that the meals and snacks for the day are posted on the cupboard door," she said calmly.

Then they both looked down at Tina's big purse, which stood open on the floor next to the refrigerator with another block of cheese sticking out of the top.

*   *   *

The next day Justin was back in his usual spot at Manning's Luxury Auto Sales, gazing out of the showroom window at the traffic passing by on the street. Suddenly a familiar form came slouching toward him across the parking lot. Hugo spotted him through the plate glass and sketched a little wave at hip level.

It was Hugo, Justin was almost sure, but the figure had lost some of its Hugo-ness. The hair, for one thing, didn't make the usual Albert Einstein-type halo around his head but was tied back neatly in a ponytail. And the antique red-and-black checked lumberjack shirt he'd been wearing all winter had been replaced by a dark green jacket. Justin recognized it as one that he had loaned Hugo several years ago and never seen again.

Hugo pushed open the door and sauntered into the showroom. "Hey, man," he asked before Justin could even say hello, "can I borrow your car?"

"My car? What's up?"

"I need to get out to the south side. Nellie's got a cousin who might have a job for me, checking new computers before they're shipped out. Think of it—getting paid to play with new computers!" He shoved out a hand, palm up. "How about it?"

"Okay, okay!" Justin looked nervously over his shoulder as he dug in his pocket and pulled out his keys. "Here. And good-bye. Old Man Manning really doesn't like us talking to anyone but customers while we're on duty."

"Consider me gone!" Hugo said cheerfully. "Thanks! I'll be back in an hour, two at the most!"

It was more than three hours later that Manning's secretary called Justin to the phone. "It's your wife!" she said breathlessly. "She sounds— Didn't you say she's expecting a baby? I think this might be it!"

Justin stood rooted to the floor. His hands fluttered helplessly in the air. "My car!" he cried. "Hugo has my car!"

"What's the matter here?" Mr. Manning stalked into the room and glared at Justin. "You're acting a bit odd, aren't you? First you disappear off the showroom floor at lunch hour and don't come back for two days—"

"Mr. Manning," the secretary cut in, "Justin's wife is having a baby and needs to go to the hospital, and Justin doesn't have a car!"

"A baby!" A sweet smile spread over Manning's face, and his eyes softened with a tender gleam. "Why didn't you say so, my boy? Will this be your first? Come, come, if it's a car you need, you're in the right place! Here, take this one," he said, reaching for a set of keys from a row of hooks behind him. "Your wife might as well ride in style. A retired businessman bought it, but he brought it back yesterday. Said it made him feel too much like a gangster. It's right out back. It's that black Jaguar."

Justin never stopped to consider whether or not the black Jaguar might be bad luck. He snatched the keys out of Manning's hand and dashed for the door. "Tell her to hold on!" he yelled back over his shoulder. "Tell her I'm on my way!"

*   *   *

It was a girl. She was born late that afternoon, big and healthy and ready to eat. They named her Sarah.

Justin was sitting on the bed next to Heather, holding Sarah. He couldn't stop looking at her: the funny little nose, the thin lines that were her eyebrows but looked more like miniature feathers, and the tiny fingers with fingernails so small that he could hardly see them, but each one perfect. With her stomach full, she was sleeping contentedly. Justin thought she was the most intelligent baby he had ever laid eyes on.

"Hello? Is it all right for you to have visitors?" called a familiar voice from the open doorway.

"Come in, Hugo," Heather said. "How polite of you to ask! Is someone coaching you on your manners?"

Hugo stepped into the room, drawing Nellie after him. Nellie's eyes lit up when she saw the baby, and her hands reached out as if they had a will of their own. "Oh, may I—" she asked softly. Justin reluctantly gave up the small, warm package that was his first-born, watching Nellie closely to be sure that she knew enough to support the baby's head. She did. She held the baby as if she had handled a hundred infants—but none so precious as this one. Hugo looked on, beaming proudly, as if he had single-handedly invented the entire scene.

"Oh, I got the job," he said casually. "Computers. Nellie's cousin. I start next week. Thanks for the loan of your car. Hey!" His mouth flapped. "Um—How did you get here?"

"In a black Jaguar," Heather said. "Only the best for our Sarah. I'm a little afraid, though, that she may have been born addicted to speed, just like her father. Justin drove so fast that we practically arrived at the hospital before we left the day care center!"

"Well, I was a just a little bit nervous," Justin admitted.

"Did everything go all right at the day care center, Nellie?" Heather asked. "When I let Tina go, I thought I would have time to replace her. I had no idea that it would mean you'd have to run things by yourself."

"I wasn't alone," Nellie murmured.

"You weren't? Who was there to help you?" Heather asked.

"Me, of course!" An enormous teddy bear bustled in through the doorway, propelled by Mrs. Grasso. "Now, where's that baby?" She handed off the teddy bear to Justin and deftly slid the baby out of Nellie's arms into her own.

"I just had a funny feeling this morning," Mrs. Grasso crooned to the baby, "and I called your mama at work, and she had just zoomed away in a fancy black car. So I figured Nellie might need a hand, and I just chugged right over there. We make a great team, Nellie and I. She talks to the children, and I take care of the parents. Right, Nellie?" she added without looking up.

Nellie smiled down at the floor. "Right, Mrs. Grasso. The Scarpellis brought Mona back to the day care center today, Mrs. Cobb, and their Luigi is getting married, so he'll have a green card."

"Nellie's just been very shy," Mrs. Grasso explained to

Heather. "But I think now that she has Hugo to look after, we're going to see a new Nellie. Oh, look, the baby's stirring! What a sweetheart!"

Justin glared at the circle of people cutting off his view of his daughter. "What we need in here is a few more people!" he humphed.

"May we come in?" called a woman's voice. Mrs. Tate appeared in the doorway with Henry Tate looming behind her. "We'll only stay a moment. Oh, look, how precious!" She scooted forward as if she was attached to a string that was pulling her toward the baby. "A girl?" she asked. "What did you name her?"

"We wanted to thank you for—for everything," added Henry Tate. He stepped forward and pumped Justin's hand. "Now that you have a little girl of your own, you'll know just how much it means to us to get our Mandy back. And we've realized—Well, we've got each other back too. We're a family again. Mandy got us to realize how important that is."

"That's great!" Justin said. But Tate had already pushed past him to try his luck at making faces at Sarah, who had decided to impress everyone by opening her eyes.

Justin sat down next to Heather again and took her hand in his. "How are you feeling?" he asked. "Think we should just grab the kid and make a getaway? I happen to know where there's a very fast car."

Heather laughed. "You're a family man now, Justin. I think you're going to find it much more difficult to disappear!"